D0925917

Ms. Ladybug and Mr. Honeybee: A Love Story at the End of Time tells the story of a ladybug and a honeybee who find each other after losing their entire families to the poisonous fogs the humans are spraying. The unlikely duo pursues a safe haven from the poisonous fog and are aided by lightning bugs, a mysterious dragonfly, and even cockroaches along the adventure of a lifetime. They encounter doubting ticks, denying termites, and a slug desperately resigned to his fate along their way, but they never give up in their seemingly hopeless quest.

Ms. Ladybug
and
Mr. Honeybee
A Love Story at the End of Time

Pauline Panagiotou-Schneider
Guy R. McPherson

Illustrations and Cover Art
Pauline Panagiotou-Schneider

America Star Books
Frederick, Maryland

© 2015 by Pauline Panagiotou-Schneider and Guy R. McPherson. All rights reserved. No part of this book may be reproduced, stored in a retrieval system or transmitted in any form or by any means without the prior written permission of the publishers, except by a reviewer who may quote brief passages in a review to be printed in a newspaper, magazine or journal.

Second printing

All characters in this book are fictitious, and any resemblance to real persons, living or dead, is coincidental.

America Star Books has allowed this work to remain exactly as the author intended, verbatim, without editorial input.

Paperback 9781635087093
Ebook 9781682297001
Softcover 9781681769288
PUBLISHED BY AMERICA STAR BOOKS, LLLP
www.americastarbooks.pub
Frederick, Maryland

With gratitude for
The Non-Human Species Who Sustain Us

ACKNOWLEDGMENTS

Big thanks to those who helped read, edit, and advise:
Anne Alexander, Suraj Kumar, Patricia Menzies,
and Sheila Merrigan

CONTENTS

INTRODUCTION

For more than 4.5 billion years the planet Earth had turned and changed and even crashed with an asteroid to form the moon from the dust of the crash. About a billion years after Earth formed, a rich variety of life began to grow. Through millions of years life evolved and died off. Throughout this seemingly endless stretch of time the Earth turned and life grew on her body, and life died on her body, and life grew again on her body. Always life would grow and then die and then grow again, wondrous and different from before, but somehow the same!

Life on Earth has always been like a wave. It comes in and it goes out, and comes in and goes out again. This journey is short compared to the journey of the universe. Earth and all the life it harbors is comprised of the dust of billions of stars that arose and blinked out within the universe we inhabit.

For the humans that lived for a blink of time, Earth was the Queen of the Universe. She was their Goddess. She was their everything. She was their mother, their father, their home, and their food. And then they killed her.

They didn't want to kill her. They just didn't know what they were doing. They didn't know that they were killing everything, including themselves! They were so excited with their inventions and powers that they did not see the harm they were causing.

The orangutans knew, and the baboons knew, and the hummingbirds knew, and especially the honeybees knew, for they were among the first to die. Some of the people tried to save them, but it was already too late.

From the early days of destruction the animals had tried to warn the humans, but the humans did not speak the animal tongues. The humans believed they were superior to the animals and therefore they did not listen to the animal languages.

Most of the humans chose not to try to understand the rest of the creatures on Earth. Humans were an odd species, although a few listened and understood their brethren. These few humans stood with the animals at the end of the Sixth Great Extinction to aid and comfort them.

The humans, too, were going extinct. There was a great sorrow across the Earth as the reality became widely recognized. At the edge of extinction, only Love remained to comfort them.

This is the story of one little Honeybee, perhaps the last one, who made a friend of Ms. Ladybug, perhaps the last of her species, at the time of this great cataclysm. It's a love story at the end of time.

The Journey Begins

M r. Honeybee had been waiting so long for his queen to return to the hive that he'd grown desperately worried and set off to find her. She had been gone for a few days and he knew her absence was not a good sign. There were hardly any nurse bees left at the hive and all the honey gatherers had disappeared. Mr. Honeybee was very worried that his hive was going to suffer collapse, as had so many other hives. It was very unusual for drones like him to leave the hive, but he loved his queen and he had to find her, no matter what.

Burdened with worry and anxious about the future, he took a big gulp of honey and a little sip of royal jelly and set off to find his queen. It was early on a summer day.

He was heartbroken as soon as his flight carried him a few meters from the hive. There were flowers deep in bloom, but no other honeybees to be seen. In one garden he saw a human wearing a mask and spraying the flowers from a bottle. He had heard from the honey gatherers that the sprays were lethal. He darted quickly away from that garden and his little bee heart quaked with fear.

He imagined his poor queen drawing her last breath after a long sweet drink of a poisoned flower. A tiny bee tear formed in his bee eye. But then he gathered his courage and forged ahead. He could not stop until he found her.

He came to a farm that he'd heard about from the honey gatherers. It was supposed to be clean and safe for them, and he hoped to find his queen there. He hoped she'd missed the poisoned garden and come here instead. He had so much hope and he crossed one of his little bee toes hoping, hoping, hoping she would be here. He was sure of it. He could feel her! He could feel her!

And then, he could smell her too!

HAPPY REUNION

He heard her unique buzzing before he saw her. Only a second later, she heard him, too. By the time their multi-faceted, compound eyes made contact, they were anxiously anticipating their reunion. You might even say they were abuzz with excitement.

In the midst of exhilaration, they nearly fell to the ground when they collided in midair. Oh, the profound joy they experienced because they were together at last!

"When Bees Collide!"

"Where have you been?" Mr. Honeybee asked. "I thought I'd never see you again. I was so worried."

"Well," the queen answered, "I became very concerned about the nurse bees and the honey gatherers. I decided to take a look around."

"Oh, no!" exclaimed Mr. Honeybee. "You should've asked one of us to go. You must not put yourself at risk."

"I know," said the queen, "but there were so few bees around. And once I was outside the hive, I became very confused."

Mr. Honeybee listened intently while studying the queen's body language. She seemed sluggish, probably because she was tired.

"We know about those nasty chemicals the humans are spraying," continued the queen, "but I'm sure there's more. I've never been so confused upon leaving the hive before. Maybe there's something in the air we don't know about."

"I'm sure there are many things we don't know about," said Mr. Honeybee. "The humans are always stringing up wires and digging trenches and kicking up dust and spewing dark-colored smoke."

"Not to mention," replied the queen, "the noise and vibrations. And it's become so dry lately."

"I know," said Mr. Honeybee. "It's hard to find flowers. The honey gatherers have to fly so far, and work so hard, just to bring back a little nectar."

"But enough about that," said the queen. "Can you take me back home? I've lost my way, and I'm *soooo* exhausted."

"Follow me, my queen. I'll have you home in a few minutes."

THE LONG ROAD HOME

The queen was faltering badly from the outset of their journey home. Mr. Honeybee encouraged her onward. "It's not far, my queen. Everybody will be so happy to see you."

Still, she struggled with every flap of her little wings. "I'm so tired. I've never felt this way before." She landed on a blade of grass.

Alighting beside her, Mr. Honeybee couldn't hide the worry in his tone. "This is a nice spot to rest. We can stay as long as you'd like."

The queen struggled to stay upright on the slim leaf of grass. She tottered, and then flapped her tiny wings to maintain her balance. "I don't know if I can make it any further."

"You're the best queen ever," said Mr. Honeybee. "There will be no hive without you. Here, I'll help you." But he quickly became paralyzed into inaction, he didn't know what to do. He dare not touch his queen for fear of hurting her.

"Oh, go on ahead," she replied. "I'll catch up later, after I get my stamina back."

"You lead, my queen. The hive is that way," he pointed in the general direction of the hive. She wheezed a few moments longer, and just when it seemed like she was done for, without another word, almost miraculously, she took flight.

Relieved, Mr. Honeybee followed the tentative, wobbly flight taken by the queen. She dipped a few times, barely staying above the ground. He shouted encouragement and gave her directions when she began to go astray.

But it was just too much. A few feet from the hive, she lost altitude and collapsed into a crumpled heap on the ground. Terrified, he landed beside her.

"My queen, my queen! We're almost home. Let me assist you." He grabbed her foreleg and began to drag her toward the hive. She whimpered, her uneven breath barely sustaining her. He dragged with all his power.

Finally, after several minutes of arduous labor, Mr. Honeybee and his beloved queen neared the hive. He paused, exhausted, inhaled deeply and held his breath. It was silent: No other bees could be heard. Even the queen had stopped breathing. Or was the wind picking up and muffling the sounds of her soft breath? He leaned closer to her, "Sweetie?" He whispered with a quivering voice and waited, barely daring to breathe himself lest he miss hearing her reply. She made no move, no response, no breath. Her large, lidless eyes stared blankly into his.

Mr. Honeybee burst into tears and fell onto her body. He cried, "No, no!" The hive was dead. His queen was dead. He wept uncontrollably at the lonely thought.

He lay there for hours at her side, nestled next to her soft, furry body. He kept thinking that maybe she was just sleeping. Maybe she would awaken and feel fine and they'd complete the last few feet to their hive. But she never moved again. Her large multifaceted eyes stared blindly up at the darkening blue sky and her silken wings rested motionless upon the soft golden fur of her thorax. Night fell, and he shivered in the cold, damp air. Finally, he slept. When he awoke to a rising sun, his blurry vision took in the horror of dead, decaying leaves. The only sounds emanated from distant tractors beginning their work of grinding up the earth. He slowly disentangled from his heroine, the queen, and covered her motionless body with a leaf.

He stared over Armageddon. The planet was dying. He could see it, hear it, and smell it. He could feel it, deep inside. He thought to himself, "Why bother going on?"

He could simply fly to the highest branch in the nearby tree and find the nearest fog. He'd heard about these fogs, the ones created by humans that spewed out their tractors and their airplanes. The humans sprayed the fog to kill insects they viewed as pests, but the fogs were lethal to all who passed through them. Mr. Honeybee would end his miserable life by flying into the nearest fog. He would join his hive and his queen in death.

As he shook his head and looked up to a high branch, a voice behind him whispered, "That's a terrible way to go. Are you sure?"

"Someone is Watching"

He spun around quickly, his eyes lighting on an orange creature slightly smaller than him. He wondered how she'd known what he was thinking. Had he spoken his thoughts out loud? "Who are you? What are you doing here?" And then, his voice shaking, "Why does it matter to you?"

Ms. Ladybug

I'm Ms. Ladybug. I saw you carrying the other bee." She stood a few inches from him on a Japanese Anemone in full bloom. "You seem very sad." He seemed upset, and she didn't want to disturb him further.

Mr. Honeybee noticed the black dots on Ms. Ladybug's orange wings. He was beginning to calm down, and her quiet demeanor helped. "How did you know what I was going to do?"

"I saw you cry. I watched as your grief overwhelmed you. I saw you look up into the tree. And I 'felt' your thoughts. Hard to explain." She paused for several seconds, and he didn't respond. She continued with a quiet voice. "I had similar thoughts when my family died. It's terrible to be alone. Such a tragedy, really."

"I'm all alone," he cried out in anguish. "Why should I live?"

Ms. Ladybug listened quietly and nodded. She gave him time to speak, and to grieve.

"I lost my hive. I lost my queen. I have no place to go. I have nothing." He sobbed and gasped for air.

After several minutes of waiting patiently while he sobbed and gasped, Ms. Ladybug finally asked, "Would you like to hear my story?"

He grew quiet. She seemed so nice. How could he say no? Mr. Honeybee focused on Ms. Ladybug, collected himself, and replied affirmatively.

"Our world is ending, sir. What's your name?" Her little voice came out smoothly, calmly, her question was more of a demand.

"Mr. Honeybee." He replied almost without thinking.

"Okay. As I said, I'm Ms. Ladybug. I've come from far away, trying to find a better place. My family and friends have all died."

That statement captured Mr. Honeybee's full attention. Suddenly he felt a kindred spirit. "Please, tell me more," he said.

"I don't remember when it started. I think it was always there. They sprayed fog from their tractors, and everybody touched by the fog died right away."

He nodded in recognition. "The fog is horrible."

"At least it's quick. Slow death is worse. My tribe died slowly. Our food, mostly small green bugs in the garden, was disappearing. I think the fog killed them. And it was so dry! The plants wilted and we were always exhausted. Eventually, my friends wilted away with the plants. They just stopped coming back."

"Yes," Mr. Honeybee said, "they stopped coming back. It was the same with my friends and co-workers, my daughters and sons. They just stopped coming back. And then my queen …" His voice trailed off, the grief plain on his face.

After a pause, she continued. "This is not the first time the patriarchal humans have caused genocide. The humans had a president named Andrew Jackson. He stuffed other humans, the indigenous ones, into boxes. They were shipped to 'reservations.' Their entire culture died. And then they died, too."

"That's terrible," Mr. Honeybee said. "How could they? And why?"

"When you believe you're superior to others, insanity ensues. You don't even know you're being insane because you don't recognize others as equals." She waited a long time before continuing. "They did the same thing to us. To my species."

"What? What do you mean?"

"They shoved us Ladybeetles into boxes and shipped us away from our homes. We arrived into foreign places and were released into gardens. But we didn't know the plants, and the plants were all dying anyway."

She paused for a few minutes. Mr. Honeybee looked very concerned. His world was tipping over, and he was discovering he wasn't alone in his suffering.

Ms. Ladybug pressed on. "We are all 'others' now. We are viewed as tools for the patriarchal humans. And when they're done with a tool, even for a few moments, they cast aside the tool. They've cast us aside, not knowing they need us to survive. The patriarchs have killed us. In doing so, they've unwittingly killed themselves."

Ms. Ladybug and Mr. Honeybee sat quietly. They heard only their own breathing. Even the tractors were silent at last. The garden he'd known his whole life was more still than a tomb.

SEEKING REFUGE

The two sat in silence for a long time, both lost in their thoughts and emotions. Finally, Mr. Honeybee said, "Thanks for telling me your story, even though it's awful. I'd rather know what's happening in the world than not know. I mean, I hate knowing. But not knowing is even worse." Then, after a long pause, "I think. But tell me, Ms. Ladybug. How do you know all this? Have your travels been that vast?"

Ms. Ladybug nodded sadly. "They have, Mr. Honeybee. I have seen many terrible things, and heard stories passed on by other survivors. The bookworms of the great human libraries have much knowledge to share with us. However, sadly, their numbers are dwindling as well because of the poisonous fogs. I had the good fortune to travel briefly with a very wise and knowledgeable, bookworm, Dr. Witsend. She shared as much knowledge as she could with me before she suffered the same fate as your lovely queen.

"The murders are continuing," said Ms. Ladybug. "As long as the patriarchs are given the reins of power, they will kill everybody else. For the most part, these patriarchs are relatively wealthy, Caucasian men. But the disease has spread to others, too. The patriarchs love this system because it gives them power. They use their power to kill everybody they can reach, which only emboldens them and increases their power."

Mr. Honeybee asked, "Is there any way to stop them?"

"I don't know. It certainly doesn't seem so. They're bloodthirsty, and seemingly addicted to the blood."

"If we can't stop them," said Mr. Honeybee, quite tentatively, "maybe we can survive their assault. Maybe our children and grandchildren will live to see better days."

"Perhaps," said Ms. Ladybug. "And we certainly must act as if that's the case. We must act as if there is a future for our kind, or there will be no future for our kind."

"Let's go," said Mr. Honeybee. "Let's try to save as many as we can. Let's spread the word about the patriarchal humans before it's too late."

And so they courageously sallied forth, into a world they couldn't know. Their mission seemed impossible, but they felt liberated by the notion of an impossible task. They knew they would die, and so would all the others, if they took no action. They probably would all die regardless of their actions. It probably wouldn't matter to any species. Nonetheless, once they had in their heads the idea of fighting, even if they couldn't possibly win, the idea of giving up seemed utterly ludicrous.

As their adventure began, and because insects and birds and humans and many other creatures are musical by nature, Ms. Ladybug broke out into a song. Mr. Honeybee learned quickly and they sang together with all their hearts.

> Imagine ... the impossible task ...
> Warning... everyone in your path ...
> Dreaming... of a place we call home ...
> Even when there's nothing to gain ...
> Carry on ... when it seems there is no point ...
> Loving all ... the unlovable ones ...
> Living as if ... there's no tomorrow ...
> Because in the end... Only love remains ...

Singing loudly, albeit with the raspy kinds of voices you would expect from untrained insects, they marched happily along. You might even say Mr. Honeybee and Ms. Ladybug had a spring in their steps (If, that is, you can picture a bee and a bug springing along as they walked, and I am most certain you are able to).

Not So Fast

Almost immediately, the odd couple encountered a fat, white termite gnawing away at the wood of a fallen tree, one of many dead trees in the field they were crossing. He ignored them while they watched him chewing at the wood, transforming the wood into tiny bits of humus. Finally, he was so distracted by their stares that he paused long enough to look up at them.

"May I help you?" he asked, clearly disgruntled by their presence.

"We were thinking that perhaps we could help each other, if possible," replied Ms. Ladybug.

"Yes, we have both recently lost our entire families and we are looking for survivors of this apocalypse," said Mr. Honeybee, a little breathlessly.

"Apocalypse? What apocalypse?" sneered the termite.

Both Mr. Honeybee and Ms. Ladybug paused at this odd question from the termite. They wondered how it was possible that this termite had remained ignorant of what was all around him. All the dead trees, for one, should have indicated that something was terribly wrong.

Mr. Honeybee had been taught proper manners of introduction and decided to try a different approach with the stranger. "Perhaps," he said, "we may introduce ourselves to you. This is my companion, Ms. Ladybug, who has traveled very far through many dangers to be here. I am Mr. Honeybee, and my hive is – or rather was – right over that knoll beyond the field of dead trees." His little voice cracked a bit as he thought of his dead hive.

His heart ached as he paused, waiting for the termite to take the hint and introduce himself. The chap, however, was clueless and slowly chewed on a piece of wood as he stared at the odd couple before him.

"Perhaps you might tell us your name?" Ms. Ladybug encouraged, catching on to Mr. Honeybee's plan.

"Who's askin'?" growled the termite between mouthfuls. Again, the couple was taken aback by the odd question. They were quite confused as to how to proceed at this point.

"Well, um, I'm Mr. Honeybee," followed by a long pause to allow the information to sink in.

"And I'm Ms. Ladybug," chirped Ms. Ladybug. "Now that we have that out of the way, again, would you be so kind as to tell us your name?" The termite was proving to be quite thick. He was, thought Ms. Ladybug to herself, as thick as wood. And she grinned just a little at the thought.

"Listen, I don't know what you two are selling, and we termites pretty much don't talk to anyone but our kind. I'm very busy and don't have time for anything else but this," the termite spoke through a mouth full of wood.

Almost together the ladybug and the bee tried to reassure the termite that they were selling nothing, that they were curious about whom the termite was, and that they had some important information to share with him. "We are not selling anything, good termite," piped up Mr. Honeybee. "But we do have some very critical and terrible news we want to share with you and see if you could help us out."

"I don't believe in terrible news. I only like good news. Or funny news," he said while chewing some more. "You got any funny news? I like that." He munched. He was not being helpful at all.

"Oh dear, oh dear, then I'll just come out and tell you," cried Ms. Ladybug. "The world as we know it is coming to an end and we are trying to save as many as we can. We're hoping many will join us in our quest for a safe place. Would you like to join us on our journey?"

"Hogwash!" spurted the termite, spraying bits of chewed wood on the couple. "Why would you say such a ridiculous thing? 'The world coming to an end,' indeed. Why, that's the stupidest thing I've ever heard! The world has never ended before!"

"That is not entirely correct, sir. The world has ended five other times, according to a very wise bookworm I encountered on this journey. May she rest in humus," Ms. Ladybug spoke self-assuredly and nodded to Mr. Honeybee, who smiled at her confidence.

"What bookworm?" snarled the termite.

"Why the notable Dr. Witsend, of course. Have you heard of her? She was based in the New York City Public Library's history section for a good number of years. She did extensive research in the natural histories and devoured several tomes on it."

"I never heard of her. And even if she existed, where is she now? And maybe she's wrong too. Don't believe everything you hear, missy." The termite was clearly agitated.

"But haven't you seen the devastation? Look at this forest! It's almost completely gone! This is an apocalypse!" Cried out Mr. Honeybee, at his wit's end.

The termite looked around at the dead trees, felled by insects and disease and storms and chainsaws. It was once a small hardwood forest, lush with oaks and ash and wild cherries, along with redbuds and hickory trees. Most of the trees were on the ground, and those still standing were obviously dead or dying. Through his termite eyes, all he saw was food, tons and tons of food. It was a windfall!

"I don't see apocalypse here, I see mountains of food. I see several years' supply of food in fact, for me and my family. I don't see devastation. I see progress!" He snapped at them.

"Now go away and leave me alone. I gots eatin' to do." And he went back to gnawing at the body of a fallen oak tree in the cemetery of a hardwood forest.

"The Trenchant Termite"

HEARTSICK AND HOMELESS

The two companions, dismayed by the dismal failure of their very first attempt to find another kindred spirit to join them, flew off, up, over, and away from the hardwood graveyard. They flew silently for a while, lost in their own thoughts, feeling the sharp sting of failure.

The warm summer breeze wafting across their little faces felt familiar, but the smells it brought were unfamiliar. They even burned a little. Everything felt foreign, alien, and terrible. A deep sadness filled their tiny hearts as they flew above the devastation. Ms. Ladybug glanced over at her new friend and saw Mr. Honeybee with tears in his eyes. His loss was still fresh and new, and his pain very evident. Her little heart went out to him. She remembered the pain she had felt losing her friends and family, one by one, one after the other. He would need to rest and eat soon, she thought. Grief must be taking its toll on him. Being an adult ladybeetle she didn't require as much food as a bee did. In fact she could go for days without food, but it was clearly evident that he could not. She looked around for a spot they could rest, perhaps a porch on a friendly home with a hummingbird feeder. Humans still put those out, even though few hummingbirds were left. They could both re-energize on the sugar water.

She flew in closer to him. "I'm so sorry, Mr. Honeybee. It's tragic knowing what we know. It's even worse that others won't listen to us."

Mr. Honeybee was grateful for her words and he replied above the noise of their wings. "I'm so lonely, Ms. Ladybug. My hive died, and knowing what we know is lonely." Another ten seconds passed before he said, "I'm glad to have met you. At least I'm not completely alone now."

Ms. Ladybug basked in the glow of his kind words. But she was conflicted, too. "I'm glad to have met you, too, Mr. Honeybee. I wish we'd have had a chance to get to know one another before-" She pondered the death of all her friends, and thought about Mr. Honeybee's loneliness. "Like, before the end of time."

He looked at her in surprise. "Do you really think this is the end of time? I mean, many have predicted our demise before. The history of prophecy is filled with errors. This might be one of those times."

"Maybe," she said. "But it's never looked this bleak before. The air is polluted. The soil is washing into the ocean. Our homes have been destroyed, time after time. We can't move fast enough to stay in front of the destruction." She watched him for his reaction, as Mr. Honeybee let her words sink in.

Then he said softly, "It does feel different to me. This time *is* different. I can feel it in the air, in the water, in the soil. Everything is dying. Everybody is dying."

In fact, he continued, "But I don't think they're just dying, Ms. Ladybug. I think they're being killed. Being murdered. I think these particular humans know what they're doing, and they're doing it anyway. I just cannot figure out why they don't see how it harms them also."

Ms. Ladybug pointed down with her slender front leg. "Look, there's a house with a hummingbird feeder. The big, yellow house with the wrap-around porch. Let's stop to rest."

WHAT'S NEXT?

The brief respite brought much-needed energy to Mr. Honeybee and Ms. Ladybug. He lapped up the sugar-water, which tasted like watered down nectar. It would suffice, but it did not replace the delicious and nutritious honey he had been raised on. The two new friends seldom spoke while lounging on the shady porch. A light, intermittent breeze wafted across their small bodies. Things almost seemed normal except that they were together and would never have been together had things been normal. Their species rarely interacted except to greet or excuse each other as they passed on a flower.

Mr. Honeybee turned to Ms. Ladybug and quietly asked, "Now what?"

Ms. Ladybug replied, "What do you mean, Mr. Honeybee?"

"That disgusting termite wasn't interested in listening to us. Why should we bother trying to tell others what we told him?"

Ms. Ladybug's face scrunched up as she thought. After a few moments, she said, "He was one. There are many. Surely some will want to know."

Instantly Mr. Honeybee shot back, "Please don't call me Shirley." Ms. Ladybug gently touched Mr. Honeybee's shoulder as they both giggled at the silly, old joke.

"We need to find a safe place to rest for the night, Mr. Honeybee. Are you ready?" He nodded in agreement and away they flew, away from the setting sun. Refreshed and growing increasingly comfortable with one another, the winged pair sought a safe place to spend the night well away from the house and its human inhabitants.

Ms. Ladybug pointed toward a large elm tree that stood tall in the fading twilight. "How's that look?"

"Good," replied Mr. Honeybee. "I'm sure I can find a crevice in the bark. I'm so tired I could sleep on a skunk's tail."

"Eww," said Ms. Ladybug, with a smile.

"While it was warding off a big dog," Mr. Honeybee followed up and he actually smiled at the shriek of laughter that came from Ms. Ladybug.

A few minutes after landing in the large tree, they settled into the craggy bark, their bodies close enough to touch each other. Ms. Ladybug turned around a few times like a dog would finding the perfect spot in a pillow and then she finally snuggled into his furry side. Mr. Honeybee didn't seem to mind. Within a few seconds, the honeybee and ladybug fell into a deep sleep.

THE DREAM

M r. Honeybee snored softly in his sleep, dreaming dreams of honey, flowers, and a large and growing family of brothers, sisters, daughters, and granddaughters. He smiled as he watched his happy hive bustling along, the older ladies dancing together while pointing out the choicest, nectar-filled flowers. Young daughters cared for new granddaughter and grandson larvae, tenderly cleaning and feeding them. Though he was not yet a father himself he moved among them feeling the warmth and joy of a father's love. He looked up from his beautiful family to see his lovely queen smiling down at him with her own heart full of love for him. It made his heart skip to see the love in her eyes. He flew to her side as she smiled at him and he followed her out of the hive where she flew high above their home.

They soared above the bustling hive, spiraling together as high as they could, she just out of reach ahead of him. Around them the trees' green foliage glistened with the blush of spring and blossoms gave up their sweet aroma. Their petals fell like rain around the two little spiraling bees. The music of birdsong filled the air and Mr. Honeybee could not imagine a better life or world. There was nothing more to desire. He reached his bee foreleg out to catch his queen's and she laughed and dodged, escaping him. He laughed and chased her harder, coming ever closer to catching his love. A shadow fell across her yellow back and it spread and he looked up to see its source. The sky, once blue and clear, was suddenly darkening and turning an ominous red. Thick, black clouds swelled and expanded, mushrooming into a menacing mass, lightning crackling in the swells and billows of the cumulonimbus clouds, sending wicked-looking fingers of light outward. Mr. Honeybee gasped and looked for his queen.

She was still rising, laughing, and somehow she did not see the danger right above her. He called out to her, but he had no voice. He tried again and still only a small croak came from his throat. He tried to fly to her, but his wings failed to carry him any higher. He felt as though a heavy weight were pulling him back to Earth, that the harder he struggled to reach his queen, the heavier he became. A blood-red rain began to pelt him and as he fought the invisible force that held him back he could see his queen soaring ever higher away from him. She looked back at him with that sweet look of love and he screamed silently as from behind her the black cloud took the form of a being with arms and legs and claw-shaped fingers and a gaping mouth filled with lightning-bolt teeth, crackling and snapping. He watched in terror as his beautiful queen was sucked into that fearsome maw and devoured into the belly of the tempest. He screamed again and this time his voice came out loud and clear and he awoke both himself and his new friend, Ms. Ladybug. She lurched from her own fitful sleep to find poor Mr. Honeybee sobbing and shaking beside her.

"Oh, my poor dear! My poor, dear, Mr. Honeybee. You are shaking so!" She wrapped a little arm around his shoulders as he shook and wept.

He sobbed, "She was right there! Right there! I tried to save her! She didn't see it!"

"There, there, my friend. Let it out. Go ahead and cry. It'll do you good." She hugged him as he wept onto her shoulder. His sad tears soaked her red-and-black spotted carapace, but she didn't seem to mind. She patted his fuzzy back and said, "There, there, dear," every now and then, and let him bury his face in her shoulder and sob. After what seemed a long time his weeping finally slowed and he leaned back to wipe the tears away. She looked intently into his face and he hesitantly looked up at her. She smiled softly at him and patiently waited.

"I'm so embarrassed." He said at last and looking around as if trying to find an escape.

"Embarrassed for what?" she asked, bemused by his words.

"For crying."

"Why would you be embarrassed for doing the most natural thing in the world?" She asked, shook her head and cocked it askew. "Would you be embarrassed for laughing your butt off at something hilarious?"

He shrugged and looked at his feet and shook his own head in the negative, adding a slow, "No, of course not."

"Well then. Why be embarrassed for crying over losing your whole family?"

"I don't know. Big boys don't cry?"

She just looked at him and said, "Everybody cries, Mr. Honeybee. Even big boys cry. Especially when they've lost everyone they love. I cried for weeks after losing my family." A tear slid down her cheek at the memory. He watched the tear roll slowly and impulsively reached out and gently wiped it away and then hugged her.

They both sat there hugging a long time without speaking, tears rolling down their cheeks, until they fell back to sleep together, in their gentle hug.

SLUGGO

Rejuvenated from their emotional release and subsequent deep sleep, Mr. Honeybee and Ms. Ladybug took flight in the morning. They didn't know quite what they were doing, or where they were going, but they still felt an urgent need to tell others what they knew. A few minutes after beginning their day's journey, Ms. Ladybug pointed down into an urban yard divided by a sidewalk running from the street to the front door of the house. "Look," she said, "there's somebody." They quickly descended and landed directly in front of a solitary slug who was pulling himself across a sidewalk.

The slug stopped and looked skeptically at the couple. He looked to the left, and then to the right, seemingly seeking a path around the bee and the bug. Finally, he said in a strong, clear voice, "May I continue, please, without going around you?" He paused for effect. "It takes me a long time to reroute my navigation."

Ms. Ladybug responded, "Please forgive us for the interruption, but we have some news of grave importance to share." The slug seemed willing to listen, so she continued, "I'm Ms. Ladybug, and this is Mr. Honeybee."

"It's a pleasure to meet you, I'm sure," said the slug. "My name is Silvestre. Everybody calls me Sluggo, though."

Mr. Honeybee joined the conversation, "It's nice to meet you, Sluggo. As Ms. Ladybug said, we have news. It's not really new, I guess, but few have noticed."

Sluggo looked confused. He looked at the bee and blinked slowly. Then he turned to look at Ms. Ladybug as he said, "Please clarify."

Ms. Ladybug looked at Mr. Honeybee, and then back at the slug. There really was no way to preface the news or frame it in an easy, digestible way, so she just blurted it out. "Our world is coming to a close. We're being killed by the patriarchal humans."

Ms. Ladybug and Mr. Honeybee were stunned when the slug threw his head back and laughed uproariously. He said, choking back additional laughter, "Of course. Of course our world is going away. Of course the patriarchs are responsible. You just noticed?"

Mr. Honeybee stammered, "We've lost our families and tribes. My hive died. We're both very sad."

"Pardon my laughter," said the slug, "but you know what they say. If you don't want to cry, you've got to laugh. And I grew tired of crying a long time ago."

"So," said Ms. Ladybug, "you know? You know about the patriarchal humans and what they're doing?"

"It's a little hard not to notice from here," said Sluggo. "I used to have a lot of room to roam. My parents and grandparents told me stories about thousands of my kind within a day's crawl from here. My world has been dissected and destroyed. The habitat has nearly vanished for me and my kind. Now there's only me, and this tiny little space, divided by the sidewalk we're sitting on. How fitting."

Ms. Ladybug fidgeted while looking first at Sluggo, and then at Mr. Honeybee. She could tell Mr. Honeybee was nervous, too. He kept shifting his gaze from the slug to the ground and back again.

"I'm sorry to sound so harsh," said Sluggo, "but as nearly as I can tell I'm in imminent danger of being the last of my kind." He let the words hang in the air, giving the ladybug and the honeybee time to absorb the message. "I can't exactly fly out of here. My food is running out. I've no place to go and no way to get there, even if there was a place for me. I'm surrounded by dry streets and drier parking lots. The adjacent lawns are filled with toxins. If the humans who live here stop watering this little patch of grass, I'll be dead in less than a week. If they remove it, I'll be gone even sooner. If you don't mind, I can't stay on this sidewalk much longer." He started moving again, directly toward Ms. Ladybug.

Stepping out of the way, she said, "I'm so sorry, Sluggo. We should have known others were suffering, too." Fumbling for words, trying to express compassion while offering hope to the slug, she asked, "What can we do? How can we help you?"

Moving slowly, Sluggo thought about the question. He overcame his first thought, which was to employ vicious sarcasm. The bug and the bee were new to the idea of habitat loss and therefore death, so he wanted to be kind. "There's nothing to be done, as much as I appreciate the offer. You can't fly me out of here on those skinny little wings, and there's no guarantee we'd find a place for me to extend my days." Nearing the end of the sidewalk and therefore entering a patch of grass, he continued, "I've had a good run. I have no complaints. I just need to keep on keeping on. Until I can't." Without looking back he said over his shiny and leopard spotted shoulder "Good luck to you."

Mr. Honeybee and Ms. Ladybug were speechless. They looked at each other as Sluggo disappeared into the grass. They had only wanted to help but there was nothing they could do. For the first time in their short lives they felt their wings were very inadequate. With heavy hearts, they took flight again. Not a word passed between them, but their minds were racing along similar paths.

LIVING HERE NOW

"We can't do anything," said Mr. Honeybee. "We can't help anybody. We're wasting our time."

"Maybe you're right, Mr. Honeybee. Maybe there's nothing we can do. Maybe we cannot help anybody. Maybe this is all a meaningless waste of time." She let the words sink in as they flew into a light breeze, the day heating up as the sun rose in the sky. "But what else are we going to do? Just give up and die?"

Mr. Honeybee let the thought roll around in his head. What else, indeed.

"Why not just give up and die? Everyone we ever loved and knew is dead. It would be easier to just end it all." He felt the tears rising to his eyes and feeling ashamed, brushed them away. Ms. Ladybug noticed and felt a pang in her heart for him.

"Mr. Honeybee, it's so easy to give up and die. But that won't change things and maybe if we can tell one other insect, bug or animal about this who gets it, well, that makes it all worth it. Doesn't it? Either way, we are damned no matter what we do. So why rush the inevitable?"

Mr. Honeybee thought, *If you're damned if you do, and damned if you don't, you might as well do.*

"Ms. Ladybug, I worry about telling everybody," the bee said. "Won't they get depressed? Or start acting badly toward each other? Won't they take instead of give?"

"Oh, Mr. Honeybee," responded the ladybug, "you've led quite a sheltered life, haven't you?"

He said, "What do you mean?"

"Have you noticed how most of them act already? There is little kindness in the world, especially between those who look differently from one another. Most already act badly toward each other." After a long pause, she continued, "Maybe if they know their lives are short – very short – they'll start behaving as if their moments together actually matter."

"Hmm," he responded, and not merely with the hum of his wings. "I suppose you're right. They *are* pretty nasty to each other." He continued, after a short pause, "Or maybe they're just trying to find their way in the world. And that takes all their time. Maybe they're seeking food and shelter and trying to survive. And maybe those pursuits simply overwhelm any positive thoughts they might have. Much less any positive actions they might take."

Ms. Ladybug was quick to respond. "Yes, I agree. Life is busy. The simple act of living leaves little time, and little energy, for anything else. But that's no excuse for thoughtlessness. We can act with decency and compassion while we live."

"Sometimes," Mr. Honeybee said, "I get to eat only because somebody else goes hungry. Sometimes there's too little of everything for everybody. Sometimes it really is a bug-eat-bug world out here."

"Of course," said Ms. Ladybug, "living takes life with its every breath. With my every breath, and with your every breath, somebody must suffer. And we are constantly in danger of being eaten ourselves by bigger bugs or animals. But that's no reason to exacerbate the suffering. It's no reason to willingly add to the suffering of others. As Carlos Castaneda once learned from the great Shaman Don Juan, you do not get offended by an attacking tiger. It is his nature."

After thinking about what Ms. Ladybug had said for several minutes, Mr. Honeybee responded: "And I guess we didn't have any choice about the time and place we were born. We just sort of showed up. We didn't say, 'I want to live here.'"

Ms. Ladybug replied, "And yet, here we are. Here. Now. Perhaps we should start living as if the moment matters. As another great wise human, Ram Dass once said, "Be Here Now." See? The humans can be wise at times."

"If we start living in the now," answered Mr. Honeybee, "the moments will start to matter."

"Now you're talking," the ladybug said.

A BRILLIANT IDEA!

"Now you're really talking," the ladybug said. "And every moment *does* matter, *has* mattered as long as there have been living beings on this planet. Poor Sluggo over there knows that more than anyone. He could dry up in a matter of moments if he took the wrong turn! Because he's so slow!" She screwed her face up as an idea began to form in her clever little brain. Mr. Honeybee thought she looked in pain and grew worried.

"Are you okay Ms. Ladybug? Did you eat something unpalatable?"

She giggled and shook her head, "Oh no, Mr. Honeybee. I always make that face when I start hatching an idea. My mother used to call me screw-face because of it."

He chuckled and then asked, "What's your idea?"

"I was thinking Sluggo is so slow and gets it, and we are so fast and it took us so long to get it. What if every moment matters, and what if lives could be saved? Should we tell the humans what they're doing to us and to them?"

"Tell the humans? Are you joking?"

"Why not at all!" She waved a slender forearm at the gradually departing form of Sluggo. "That little fellah gave me the inspiration and idea that we've been missing. We should go to the source of who is murdering us!"

"Oh Ms. Ladybug. That's a noble idea, but humans cannot speak our languages and even though we understand the humans, we can't speak human! How in the world could we ever communicate with them? Let alone explain such a complex idea as," and he made a silly pompous face and voice as he spoke, "*Hey you guys are killing us, and in the process are killing yourselves too, you should stop!* Okay, have a nice day!"

Ms. Ladybug just smiled confidently back at him. "I speak Morse code!"

"You speak what?"

"Morse code. It's a universal language of communication that requires the mere beeping of a tone. There are long beeps and short beeps and the most common phrase used, which was taught me by Professor Witsend, the wise and learned bookworm, is SOS. Apparently it means Save Our Souls. Some humans have a belief in the after-life and in the soul, a kind of energy that comes out of their bodies upon dying, and which then lingers a bit before going on to wherever it is supposed to go. It's all very complicated and philosophical and changes from culture to culture, but they love their souls and when they are in dire straits, they cry out SOS! They send Morse code messages through electrical surges that float on the air like the electromagnetic waves that birds use to navigate. Were we to use the SOS language, I'm certain they'd understand and realize that we are sentient beings and have lives and hopes and dreams, too. Albeit on a smaller, shorter-lived, much faster scale."

Mr. Honeybee was confused by the stream of words emitting from Ms. Ladybug's mouth. He just stared at her in utter disbelief. She noticed and crossed her arms impatiently.

"Am I going too fast for you?"

He nodded slowly, "A little bit. Though I'm not sure if slowing down will make a difference." He thought for a moment, as she seemed frustrated with his inability to grasp what she was saying. "How would you use this Marsh code with the humans?"

"*Morse* code, not Marsh code. And I'm not sure yet. We would need a way to create a noise that could be understood by a human brain." She shook her head in dismay, "They have such large heads, and they rarely use them. Such a waste of good space."

"Well," said Mr. Honeybee, "what does the SOS signal sound like? Perhaps we could ask a bird to chirp it for us?"

"That's a fine idea!" She grew excited at the suggestion. "The sound is three short beeps, three long beeps, and three short beeps."

Mr. Honeybee thought a moment and then buzzed out three short buzzes, three long buzzes, and then three short buzzes. "Like that?"

"Yes!! Exactly! You speak Morse code?"

"No, of course I do not, but you described it so well, that even a fool like myself could understand," he teased her.

"Perhaps even a *human* fool!" She teased back and did a little flip in mid-air, which made him laugh. And then he imitated her flip and soon they were flying through the air flipping and laughing and looking for a human that might be intelligent enough to understand Morse code.

They passed several humans that looked potentially intelligent enough, but Ms. Ladybug was looking for a very special kind of human. She believed that a human that could communicate in several languages might be their best hope. Soon they came upon a bus stop where there were several people gathered waiting for a bus. She and Mr. Honeybee alighted on the glass enclosure of the bus stop and listened to the various conversations taking place. There were people of different colors, and sizes and shapes, adult people and children people, several very old people. It was still morning and many were heading to work and had a tired look in their eyes. Mr. Honeybee felt sorry for them.

He knew how much humans loved his species' honey and royal jelly, and how good it was for them. For thousands of years, perhaps even millions, humans had lived beside honeybees in harmony. Now that relationship was over because some of the humans had become greedy and tried to force more out of a planet that could only give so much.

Ms. Ladybug had found her perfect human, a mother with a young child was talking to a human next to her in a strange language and then to her child of about 9 years of age in a completely different language, the language that was most spoken in this part of the world. Ms. Ladybug nudged Mr. Honeybee in the direction of the woman and child.

"They're the ones! They are our last, best hope! They speak multiple languages and are most likely able to understand Morse code!" She was getting very excited now, and he was getting very nervous. He knew very well how little humans tolerated bees, despite the fact that bees rarely stung humans. Bees were always blamed for the crimes of wasps and hornets who indiscriminately stung people all the time. Such nasty cousins and then he snickered to himself and thought: *Who can blame them? Humans deserve stinging especially with how they've been behaving. I'd sting them all if I could.* He paused and remembered one kind human. *Except for my beekeeper. He was very kind. He wept outside our hive as he noticed our numbers were dwindling. He tried to save us.* Mr. Honeybee choked back a tear. Ms. Ladybug pulled him out of his reverie and thrust him into the face of the woman who spoke many languages.

"There! Do it Mr. Honeybee! Do the SOS signal!" She cried out and Mr. Honeybee, startled into action, began to buzz frantically in front of the woman's face.

The scream was heard three blocks away and caused several people to pause in their tracks and wonder who was being murdered and by what. Several people, certain a murder was taking place, dialed 911 to report the bloodcurdling scream to the police, Mr. Honeybee had caused quite a commotion in the little bus stop. Humans were running in all directions, arms flailing, and people screaming to get out of his way. There was something about this little bee that they could not make it go away! It so easily dodged their waving arms and bags and newspapers. The humans were convinced that the little bee was out to kill them all, and sting them all to death. Their large brains had convinced them of that, even though it would be physiologically impossible for one little bee to sting one of those people to death, let alone all of them. Such a bee would die at the first sting and it would all be over for him. It goes against such a bee's instinct to sting humans indiscriminately. Stinging was meant as a last resort to protect the hive against invaders, who most often were those nasty yellow jackets that were always trying to steal their honey. Honeybees and humans had a mutual enemy in the yellow jackets. Besides, he was a male bee and had no stinger at all. It was all really a huge misunderstanding.

He realized that the woman he was trying to communicate with was wholly unresponsive to his message. Her screams drowned out his buzzes and so she was not able to understand what he was trying to tell her. Not to mention that the other people continually interrupted his beeping attempts by trying to swat him. It made it very difficult to complete even half of the message. But he was determined and finally had managed to buzz out SOS at least five times in front of her, without interruption, while her 9-year-old watched him silently and grinned at the adults that were in a general freak-out mode and making fools of themselves over a tiny drone honeybee.

Ms. Ladybug had stayed safely out of the way perched on the glass and watched in horror as the events unfolded. From her safe perch, she dodged and weaved sympathetically with every dodge and weave Mr. Honeybee made, covering her eyes in horror as a newspaper came swatting down in his direction. She peeked from behind her forelimbs and saw Mr. Honeybee still intact and still struggling to share the message. She immediately regretted this idea and felt awful to have placed him in such a dangerous situation. She noticed that the woman's child tugged at her sleeve and was trying to tell her something. The mother was too terrified to even acknowledge her child's existence. The honeybee that was acting so bizarrely would not go away!

"But mom! It's just a honeybee, it won't sting you!"

More screams and swattings ensued as the child was simply ignored. Ms. Ladybug shook her head sadly.

"Mr. Honeybee Wreaks Havoc in the Bus Stop!"

Finally Mr. Honeybee was growing tired of this adventure and the danger seemed to be escalating to a new level as more people seemed to be sprouting newspapers from their arms. He decided to beat a hasty retreat and with one last buzz, turned and zipped out of the bus stop with Ms. Ladybug hot on his tail.

As they soared up and away to go rest on a tree limb nearby, Mr. Honeybee and Ms. Ladybug could just barely make out hearing from behind them the small voice of the woman's child saying, "Mom, he was buzzing Morse code! He was buzzing SOS!"

And the mother shouted back at him, "Stop making up these stories, Guillermo! You cannot talk to the animals or the bugs! And they cannot talk to you! I was nearly murdered by that bee! I'm going to take you to the shrink! He'll fix you once and for all."

The two little traumatized bugs sat on the branch overlooking the still-panicked humans in the bus stop. The two bugs sat for a long time quietly, not exchanging any words. After a while Ms. Ladybug felt the need to speak up, perhaps prematurely. "That went well! Don't you think?" Ms. Ladybug chirped half-heartedly. "The boy understood ...." Her words trailed off.

Mr. Honeybee slowly turned his head to look at her. He said nothing and looked back at the scene of insane humans below.

"I guess it could have gone better." She muttered and sighed. Mr. Honeybee remained silent, grateful that he'd survived her brilliant idea.

"No more brilliant ideas, please." He said softly, still making sure all his limbs were intact. "I'd like to live to see the sun set."

INTO THE FOG

While resting in a dying oak tree, Mr. Honeybee and Ms. Ladybug talked long into the afternoon about how they ought to spend their time. Shall they sound the alarm to others, or simply seek a place to maximize their days? Perhaps some combination of the two would prove satisfying.

Time sped by as they enjoyed each other's company. The riveting conversation of plans and dreams distracted them from the high temperature, the setting sun, and even from the pangs of hunger digging into their tiny bellies. Upon noticing the late hour, they hurriedly gathered themselves and headed into the dimming twilight, suddenly anxious for a safe place to spend the night. The dying oak did not have enough leaves to protect them from evening predators or the frequently unpredictable weather. The wind was in their faces, and it had quickened since earlier in the day. They flew near the ground, where the wind was weakest, to save their strength.

"Another tree like last night would be nice," said Ms. Ladybug. "The rough bark makes it easy for me. I do like it rough."

"And I like the tight crevices in the bark," added Mr. Honeybee. "Easy to hide in from bigger bugs."

"There's nothing around here, that's for sure," she said, her voice quaking enough that Mr. Honeybee noticed. Indeed, they were surrounded by a concrete city with patches of dying trees in abandoned lots filled with rubble and wild scrub. Gone were the spontaneous gardens of the past that people had taken upon themselves to grow organic food and flowers in the abandoned lots. Those little garden oases of the past were cherished dreams to city bugs like Ms. Ladybug. They had all been banished now as the land owners took claim of those patches, chased out the gardeners, and then, after all, let them sit abandoned to collect garbage and spare rubble from other building projects.

Tired, hungry, and feeling weak, they crested a hill. Immediately they were overcome with confusion. The fog! They'd flown into the fog!

Ms. Ladybug wailed as she plummeted to the ground. Mr. Honeybee saw her go down, and tried to follow her. He couldn't breathe. He panicked and, like Ms. Ladybug, he fell to the ground. He couldn't see her. He couldn't hear her. He was dazed and disoriented.

Once he was on the ground the air was clearer. He could breathe again, albeit with difficulty. He was afraid to fly up into the fog, which was hanging over his head as far as he could see. But he had to find Ms. Ladybug. Even though they'd known each other only for a short time, somehow he felt he couldn't go on without her in his life.

Ms. Ladybug was only a few feet away from Mr. Honeybee, but she was confused, too. She knew they'd flown into the fog, but she lost track of everything that followed. She was on the ground, on her back, looking up into the fog. She could breathe, but she didn't know where to go. And, much to her chagrin, Mr. Honeybee was no longer by her side.

They stumbled about, each of them afraid to leave the ground and fly into the fog. Each of them lacked coordination for walking across the lumpy ground. Night was falling quickly.

Ms. Ladybug's plaintive cries went unheard. "Mr. Honeybee? Help! Are you there?"

Although he was only a few feet away, Mr. Honeybee could not hear her. Her voice simply wasn't loud enough. And she couldn't hear him, either. "Ms. Ladybug? Where are you?"

Ms. Ladybug rested on the ground, taking in deep breaths as the fog lifted. She couldn't stay here. It was too dangerous. But she couldn't leave without Mr. Honeybee. And she had no idea where he was, or even if he was alive.

Mr. Honeybee was annoyed with himself. He stumbled across the cloggy soil, looking into the impenetrable darkness. He'd let her fall away, and now she was lost. He might never see her again. The thought instantly brought tears to his eyes, and he fell to the ground, sobbing.

Ms. Ladybug looked up into the sky, hoping the moon would rise high enough to light her way. Instead, she saw dozens of twinkling lights. The stars, perhaps?

Mr. Honeybee recovered temporarily from his weeping and looked into the sky. He knew he had to gain altitude. He couldn't spend the night here. Had the fog cleared enough? Like Ms. Ladybug, he saw dozens of twinkling lights. Like Ms. Ladybug, he failed to recognize them most likely from the mild effects of the fog on their cognitive faculties.

After a few seconds, they both knew the source of the twinkling lights. Fireflies! They'd seen them before, albeit rarely of late.

The fireflies descended upon Ms. Ladybug and Mr. Honeybee. Within moments, the two were reunited with a little help from their new friends. A few minutes later, carried by the sprinkle of fireflies, they had settled into the gnarly bark of an ancient oak tree still struggling along.

Stunned by what had happened, they hugged each other in desperate relief.

"Ms. Ladybug, I thought I'd never see you again!" He whispered into her shoulder as they hugged.

"My dear Mr. Honeybee, I feared as much as well!"

"I am so happy you're not dead!" He cried out, now staring into her sparkling black eyes that threatened to burst into tears again. They smiled at each other as warm feelings of joy spread through their bodies. There were other feelings, too, and they were wonderful but impossible to describe.

Safely snuggled into the crevices of the bark, they faded into their dreams. As they nodded off, they saw dozens of twinkling lights reflecting in the small stream that flowed beneath them.

MAKING PLANS AND
THINKING OF THE FUTURE

They were still exhausted when they awoke the next day. They stirred often during the night and, each time, they looked to make sure the other was there. Finally they stretched with contentment as they prepared to start their day. The sun was already high in the sky.

"Our new friends will be here in a few hours," said Ms. Ladybug. The fireflies had promised to return at twilight.

"I can't wait to see them again," said Mr. Honeybee. "I didn't understand everything they said. I was so confused and tired when they left."

"Me, too," said Ms. Ladybug. "I think the fog clouded our abilities to think clearly. Plus, I was exhausted, and they were in a hurry. Did I actually hear them mention a safe place? Or did I dream that?"

"I think so," said Mr. Honeybee. "That's what I think I heard too. They talked about a safe place. It has some sort of dome. Or maybe it's underground. And it's filled with all sorts of creatures. The humans don't use the fog."

"Or any other poisons," Ms. Ladybug added.

"It sounds like paradise," Mr. Honeybee said with a sigh.

"Not to change the subject," Ms. Ladybug said in her typically upbeat tone, "but why *are* these humans killing everything? Are they are afraid of us? Do they hate us?"

"I've thought about that for a long time," said Mr. Honeybee. "I suspect most of them are ignorant: They know not what they do. And I imagine they prefer ignorance because it allows them to forgo responsibility. They seem to be happy enough, so they carry on as if there's nothing wrong. For most of them, there *is* nothing wrong. They studiously ignore death and destruction and, in return, they get food and water and a nice place to live."

Ms. Ladybug cried out, "How can they not see what's happening? Are they blind?"

Mr. Honeybee thought before answering, "Yes, they are blind. They have been blinded by comfort. They are too comfortable. They have food and water. They have homes. They hurry around from place to place, blinded to reality by the illusion of their make-believe lives. They watch the world through noisy, artificial lenses attached to the walls of their caves."

"But still," interrupted Ms. Ladybug, "they must know what they're doing."

"At some level, I'm sure they know," said Mr. Honeybee. "But it's easier for them to pursue baubles than to see the reality about how they live. Knowing your actions are lethal to others is a heavy burden. Not thinking about it is, well, easier. Remember our conversation with that termite?"

Ms. Ladybug shot back, "How could I forget? What a horrible creature."

"He doesn't feel that way," said Mr. Honeybee. "He's blissfully ignoring everything beyond his own immediate needs and desires."

Ms. Ladybug sputtered, "How? How can he ignore all the damage he's causing?

"Technically, he didn't kill the trees, and I doubt he sees using them all up as damage," said Mr. Honeybee. "He might not see it at all. Like many of the humans, I think he's incapable of seeing very far."

"I agree," said Ms. Ladybug. "He can't see what havoc he wreaks. He can't see beyond his nose. He can't predict what will happen in five seconds, much less what will happen to future generations." She paused and then continued, "He can't even see that those dead trees WILL RUN OUT!"

"It's all so very sad," Mr. Honeybee said. "All of it: the ignorance, the greed, the short-sighted pursuits. It's a mess."

"Yes, Mr. Honeybee, it's a mess. Not one of our making, either. We didn't create this mare's nest, but we're trapped in it. Do you believe we'll find a way out?"

"I don't know if there is a way out," said Mr. Honeybee. "But I sure am glad to be looking for it with you because I think we must act as if there is. We must act as if we can find a nice place, and not just for us, but for future generations. Maybe the fireflies can take us there."

"That's a nice thought. Maybe we'll find out this evening."

Mr. Honeybee said, "Speaking of this evening, we'd better find something to eat. I don't want to have another accident like yesterday and I'm feeling quite faint."

"We certainly do NOT."

They Called It Paradise

As promised, the assemblage of fireflies appeared at twilight. Mr. Honeybee and Ms. Ladybug were adequately fed and somewhat rested when they arrived.

"Greetings," said one of the fireflies. "My name is Eubuleus, and I am the elder of this group." He nodded toward the twinkling lights behind him.

"Hello, I'm Ms. Ladybug, and this," she said, pointing her front leg, "is Mr. Honeybee. Thank you so much for rescuing us last night."

"I don't know what we'd have done in your absence," affirmed Mr. Honeybee. "I've never been so scared."

"Our timing was good, that's all," replied Eubuleus. "We are happy to help when we can." His retiring demeanor matched his humble words.

"We were quite tired when you left us last night," said Mr. Honeybee. "Too tired, really, to comprehend what you were saying. Will you start over?"

"Yes," said Ms. Ladybug, "from the beginning, please?"

Their comments elicited only a blank stare from the firefly. Ms. Ladybug realized their questions needed context, so she added, "About the safe place."

"The place without the fog," said Mr. Honeybee. "It sounds wonderful."

"Oh, that," said Eubuleus. "We've heard about this place, but we've not been there ourselves."

"Please," implored Mr. Honeybee, "tell us more. What have you heard? Where is it? How can we find it?"

Eubuleus blinked on and off for a few moments while looking at the other fireflies. Shortly thereafter, they began blinking back. Soon there was a cacophony of blinking lights, eerily accompanied by silence. Eubuleus watched, clearly concentrating to remember the messages. Finally he turned to Mr. Honeybee and Ms. Ladybug.

"It's little more than a rumor at this point. We've heard conflicting accounts regarding its location and condition. The most reliable sources indicate it's two or three day's flight from here, near the highest peaks." He nodded in the general direction of the mountains.

Mr. Honeybee and Ms. Ladybug looked at each other, clearly disappointed. They'd hoped for much better news based on the bits they'd heard before exhaustion overtook them the night before. "So there's no dome?" Mr. Honeybee asked.

Eubuleus shook his head in the negative. "Is it underground?" Asked Ms. Ladybug, tentatively. Again the firefly shook his head solemnly.

After an uncomfortably long pause, Ms. Ladybug said, "I guess we got our hopes up." Her voice was so soft Mr. Honeybee could hardly hear her words. "We desperately want to escape the ravages of the patriarchal humans. Is there no place to go?"

"It seems," said the firefly, "most humans have a severe case of cranio-rectal inversion." Mr. Honeybee and Ms. Ladybug smiled as all the fireflies lit up simultaneously. "Apparently they are unwilling to admit that killing us leads to their own deaths. They don't understand the interconnected nature of life."

"We do *so* much for them," Mr. Honeybee commiserated. "Imagine what they'd eat, if not for us."

"I know," said Eubuleus. "We all know you pollinate much of their food. And we lightning bugs provide important services in controlling insect population. Our young are voracious eaters of plant eating bugs. You'd think they'd give us a little room to live. Instead, they seem intent upon determining how many of us they can live without."

"Sorry to change the subject," said Ms. Ladybug, "but I'd like to try to find that place. We're certain to die if we stay here, and that includes all our descendants, too. Moving elsewhere is dangerous, and we're almost certain to die along the way regardless. And the place we're seeking may not even exist." Her voice trailed off sadly.

"You sound very enthusiastic about seeking another place," said Mr. Honeybee, his voice dripping with sarcasm as he smiled.

"Well," responded Ms. Ladybug, channeling Mr. Honeybee's earlier thoughts, something insects are very good at doing, "if you're damned if you do, and damned if you don't, then we may as well *do*. I don't see much point sitting around waiting to die. And that's exactly where we're headed if we stay here. Instead of waiting to die, let's live. Let's act as if our actions matter. Eventually, perhaps they will."

"If not for us, then maybe for others." added Mr. Honeybee. "Let history judge us kindly."

"Assuming we have a history," said Ms. Ladybug.

"You know," drawled the honeybee, "it's all about perspective, if you ask me." He paused and the only sound was of crickets chirping. Unimpeded, he continued, "We can take the perspective that it's not an apocalypse, it's an adventure!" Crickets.

"Everyone's a critic," he sighed.

Eubuleus blinked back and forth with the other fireflies for a few minutes. He turned to the duo at last, "We're willing to lead the way, based on the limited information we have at our disposal. We'd like to start now, if you're ready."

Mr. Honeybee made eye contact with Ms. Ladybug and together they nodded their heads in agreement. "Let's go," she said in a calm, resolute voice.

"Very good. Away!" cried Eubuleus and hundreds of lightning bugs lit up and rose like a cloud with Mr. Honeybee and Ms. Ladybug in the midst of them.

FLY BY NIGHT

The fireflies were accustomed to flying all night, and after a day of rest they seemed to have the ability to fly forever. However, Mr. Honeybee and Ms. Ladybug, already taxed by their grief, their wearisome travels, and a night of fitful sleep, grew tired and began to fall behind as morning approached. Luckily Eubuleus noticed and sent a scout back for them to herd them back into the cluster of lightning bugs along with a stern warning to stay close for safety.

Only a shared sense of determination and frequent encouragement between the two of them allowed them to stick with the group of fireflies as the rosy-fingered dawn broke in the eastern sky.

TICKED OFF

They slept fitfully during the day. Unlike the fireflies, Mr. Honeybee and Ms. Ladybug were accustomed to sleeping under dark skies. Sleeping under a blinding sun on a warm day was terribly unsettling.

They finally gave up trying to sleep just in time to see a deer tick amble through the blades of grass. Tired and grumpy, Mr. Honeybee concluded there would be no disadvantage to engaging the tick in conversation.

"Greetings, fellow traveler," called out Mr. Honeybee from his lofty perch above the ground-crawling tick. The tick looked left and right, but not up. She looked confused. "I'm up here, above you, on this leaf," said Mr. Honeybee.

The deer tick's tiny head swiveled upward. "What do you want?"

Mr. Honeybee put on his most compassionate look. He tried to soften his eyes and his heart as he said, "I want to help. We want to help. I'm Mr. Honeybee and this is Ms. Ladybug." He gestured toward his friend.

"Thanks, but no thanks. I'm getting along just fine. If you'll excuse me, I need to find dinner."

"We know you don't need us," Ms. Ladybug said in the kindest tone she could muster. "And we certainly don't want to delay your dinner. Do you mind if we accompany you? We promise to stay out of your way."

"Do what you want," said the deer tick. "I don't suppose I can stop you from going where you want. Just try not to scare off my dinner. I haven't eaten in three years and I'm hungry enough to take a bite of you two."

Mr. Honeybee and Ms. Ladybug flew the short distance to the ground and walked alongside the tick. "We didn't catch your name," said Ms. Ladybug, with a politely questioning tone.

"That's because I didn't give it," said the tick. "I don't imagine we'll be spending much time together. There's no reason to get all cozy. The next furry thing walks by and I'm out of here."

"As you wish," said Ms. Ladybug. "What we have to say might surprise you. We think the state of the world is quite alarming."

"Um hmm," said the tick as she steadily marched through the grass towering over the three of them.

"We've noticed a sharp decline in our numbers," said Mr. Honeybee. "Furthermore, we're rapidly running out of places to live."

"Sounds like a personal problem to me," sneered the tick. "I've still got plenty of hosts to provide my food. In fact, I do believe it's easier than ever to find my prey."

"But," said Mr. Honeybee, before he was interrupted by the tick.

"I'm not done," said the tick. "As far as declining numbers, I can't say I noticed. I don't spend a lot of time at parties, so maybe you're right. But I don't really care, so long as I've got plenty of food. And lately I'm finding plenty of food." She glared at the two travelers and then pointed at them with her leg for emphasis, "*Plenty!*"

After a lengthy pause to make sure the tick was finished speaking, Mr. Honeybee said, "The point is that declining numbers are indicating something is wrong. Many of us are noticing sharp declines in our numbers. We think our homes are being destroyed. We believe we may all be facing extinction."

"I've heard that kind of talk my entire life," said the tick. "These things always go in cycles. Some years there are lots of us. Other years, not so many. I don't see where it's anything to worry about. And there's nothing we can do about it, anyway."

"We have reason to believe," said Ms. Ladybug, "that this time is different."

"Bah," said the tick with disdain. "It's always different. Sometimes it's your cousin. Eventually it's you. But nobody gets out alive, do they?"

"Of course not," said Mr. Honeybee, frustration creeping into his voice. Ms. Ladybug shot him a glance of warning, and reached out with her foreleg to pat him on the shoulder. "But we'd like to ensure the best possible future for our kind, and yours, too. The humans in charge of death and destruction apparently have other plans for us."

"I like to chew on humans," said the tick. "They're easy to catch, and they don't even notice when I'm sucking the blood out of 'em. I try to stay focused on the day-to-day stuff. This gives me plenty of time to kick back and relax. I just need a meal now and then. So far, I haven't missed a lot of meals and I can wait a long time between meals even if the numbers dwindle, as you say. I'm not gonna let a couple fearmongers scare me with some story. Ticks will never go extinct. Ya hear me? Never!"

Ms. Ladybug asked, "What will you eat when the humans and other animals disappear?"

"Ha! Are you kidding? There are humans everywhere. Last I heard, there were more being added every day. The last thing I'm worried about is running out of humans. And if the humans all disappear, there are plenty of other animals and other critters to chew on: deer, rabbits, cows, horses, and a bunch of furry squirrels and such-like. And if those run out, I'll adapt. Maybe I'll suck on your types! Bwahahahahaaa!"

The tick's laughter startled the two gentle souls and they pulled away from the tick and her bawdy laughter.

Mr. Honeybee and Ms. Ladybug could tell the tick wouldn't listen to them. She believed she could ride out any catastrophe and even adapt to a world with no food. They were disappointed, but they bid adieu to the tick with no name.

"That was a royal waste of time," said Mr. Honeybee to Ms. Ladybug when the tick was out of earshot.

"She was a royal pain in the ..." Ms. Ladybug's comment was cut off by Mr. Honeybee.

"This whole save-the-world thing isn't very rewarding." He groused.

"I know, Mr. Honeybee. But we can't give up."

"Why not? If nobody wants to know, why do we keep bothering telling them?" He kicked a tiny pebble in disgust.

Ms. Ladybug thought for a moment before answering, "I don't believe nobody wants to know. I have to believe there are others like us and the fireflies."

"I suppose. I mean, we met the fireflies, and they're awesome."

Ms. Ladybug said, "Oh, yes! We have friends, and they're leading us on this adventure. They don't need to do it. They rescued us and they believed us. Now we have their support."

"And I think we're getting better, too," said Mr. Honeybee. "Even though the tick didn't listen, we didn't lose our composure. I'm getting better at listening."

"We're both getting better, Mr. Honeybee. We won't get through to everybody, and probably not even to very many. But we're more compassionate and less pushy than we were only a couple days ago." She smiled at him, "We're becoming better beings." He smiled back.

"If we don't change a single mind beyond ours, if we don't cause a single individual to act beyond ourselves, if we fail completely to convince anybody of anything, we still haven't failed. Because we've changed ourselves." He said in agreement.

Ms. Ladybug burst into tears. Blubbering through her tears, she said, "That's so beautiful, Mr. Honeybee. And it's perfect."

Mr. Honeybee reached out his forelegs to Ms. Ladybug. She leaned into him, and he hugged her tightly. Their bodies rocked peacefully for nearly an hour without a word.

"Oh, Ms. Ladybug. Twilight is upon us. We need to find our new friends. They'll be ready to go soon. I'm hungry again." He complained sullenly and she patted his round belly while smiling at him.

"We'll fill it up soon. No worries." She comforted him.

GROGGY BEGINNINGS

The fireflies were gathering to leave for their second day of travel when Mr. Honeybee and Ms. Ladybug arrived back at the camp. Within minutes, the unlikely ensemble took flight.

Rumors among the fireflies had them arriving at their destination tomorrow. They could hardly wait. Their anticipation was nearly palpable enough to overwhelm their exhaustion. Nearly, but not quite.

The night was much like the one before. They worked hard to cover a long distance, taking little time to rest and none to eat. The fireflies were steady travelers, communicating very little as they flew in tight formation at a modest speed. They had a hive mind that kept them together, moving like a single organism, riding the evening winds, dodging the cross-breezes. Mr. Honeybee and Ms. Ladybug again struggled to keep up, and again collapsed into fitful sleep upon arrival at the day's destination. They were poorly suited for nocturnal lives.

Again they groggily arose before sunrise. Again the fireflies were sleeping comfortably.

Ms. Ladybug looked at Mr. Honeybee and asked, "How do they do that?"

"It must be something they're drinking," replied Mr. Honeybee with a smile.

"Well, we'll need to get some of that," said Ms. Ladybug.

"Whatever *that* is, *I* need to get some ASAP!" jibed Mr. Honeybee and began to search for food with Ms. Ladybug staying nearby.

After a while Mr. Honeybee's tone became serious. "What do you think about this trip, Ms. Ladybug? Are we chasing false hope?"

Ms. Ladybug took a few seconds to respond and, when she did, her voice was quiet but resolute. "I don't think there's any other kind, Mr. Honeybee. I think all hope is misguided."

Mr. Honeybee responded with surprise. "What? I've never heard that before. I thought hope was part of keeping a positive outlook."

Ms. Ladybug again let a few seconds pass before responding. "I'm unconvinced a positive outlook is any kind of solution. I think hope and wishful thinking are the same things. I think they've been pushed upon us by culture, much as 'thinking positive' has been pushed upon us. I no longer have 'faith' in these terms."

"But we can't give up hope," pleaded Mr. Honeybee.

"Why not? What's so great about hope? What's so great about wishful thinking? What's so great about keeping a positive attitude? Why don't we embrace reality instead?"

Mr. Honeybee was dumbstruck. Sitting in a crevice in an old elm tree, he muttered to himself as he tried to incorporate Ms. Ladybug's reasonable perspective with an entire life of cultural indoctrination. It wasn't going well, as Ms. Ladybug could tell from the muttering and body language.

"I mean," Ms. Ladybug said, "I don't understand the point of hoping, despite what we've been told over and over again. I'm all for wishing upon stars, but I'm no longer convinced the wishing will solve anything. In fact," she said, reflecting upon the idea for the first time, "I suspect believing in hope is making matters worse, not better."

"How could that be? How could hoping hurt?"

"By depending on that hope," said Ms. Ladybug. "Believing in hope is analogous to believing in fairy tales and magic. It's no path forward."

"Okay," said Mr. Honeybee, tentatively.

"Let's not depend upon hope and wishful thinking and fairy tales. Let's depend upon ourselves."

"How do we do that? How do we abandon positive thinking and still muddle ahead?" Mr. Honeybee was clearly unconvinced.

"As I said," repeated Ms. Ladybug, "by depending upon ourselves. We need to take action, which is what we're doing, instead of hoping and wishing. Relying on faith and hope is counting on others to do the heavy lifting. I don't want to hear how positive thinking and wishing and hoping and — goddess forbid, praying — are going to get us out of every single predicament. There is no *Deus ex machina* in the real world."

Mr. Honeybee sat in stunned silence, his tiny brain working overtime.

"There is no higher power," continued Ms. Ladybug, now quite comfortable with her soliloquy. "There is no savior on the horizon. There is no 'other.' There is no nirvana. There is no future. There is only us. There is only here. There is only now."

"But," stammered Mr. Honeybee, "what about …" his voice trailed off.

Ms. Ladybug did not respond. Instead, she let her words sink in, and played them over in her head. She hadn't planned to say any of that. It just burst out of her. But she didn't mind what she'd said. If fact, the more she pondered what she'd said, the better she liked it. It felt honest.

Mr. Honeybee still wasn't so sure. But he dipped his toes into the intellectual pool Ms. Ladybug had created. "Action, then," he said. "Action it is. Action by us. Action by us right now. Action by us, right here and now."

"We'll need to wake the fireflies before we accomplish much of anything," Ms. Ladybug said with a little giggle and Mr. Honeybee smiled at her until his tummy growled at him.

"I need to find food!"

"Hungry?"

"Yes!"

"Again?"

"Always!"

HERE BE DRAGONS

They were interrupted by the buzz of a beautiful, blue-and-yellow dragonfly. It hovered nearby, looking curiously at the ladybug and the honeybee. Finally it spoke. "I haven't seen your kind together before. In fact, I haven't seen many of either of you for quite a while. Correction. I haven't seen either of your kind. At all. For a very long time."

Mr. Honeybee and Ms. Ladybug looked at the dragonfly, and then at each other. Ms. Ladybug piped up, "Thanks for dropping by. I'm Ms. Ladybug, and this is Mr. Honeybee."

"It's a pleasure to meet you," said the dragonfly. "I'm Lozan, daughter of Geronimo and Alope." As if suspended from a string, she hovered without changing position. Paradoxically, her wings moved too fast to see. "As I was saying," she continued, "I've not seen any ladybugs or honeybees around here lately. What brings you to the neighborhood?"

"We're on a quest," said Mr. Honeybee. "We're traveling with a group of fireflies. They heard about a safe place, and they are leading us there."

Lozan asked, "Safe from what?"

"The fog," said Mr. Honeybee. "And other poisons, too. We're rapidly running out of places to live. The clean water is disappearing, along with our food."

"The humans are killing us," said Ms. Ladybug. "At least, the subset of humans who exert primary control. And we fear they are killing everybody else, too."

"Even themselves," said Mr. Honeybee.

"I've observed them for a long time," Lozan said. "I fear you're correct. They don't know what they're doing to us. They don't even know what they're doing to themselves." After a pause and a quick look around, Lozan continued, "Where's this place you're headed? Are there humans there?"

"We don't know exactly where it is. It's supposed to be a day's flight that way," Mr. Honeybee said, pointing with his foreleg.

"We don't know much about it at all," Ms. Ladybug said. "If there are humans there, then they understand how to get along with others."

"That's what we've heard, at least," Mr. Honeybee added.

Lozan pondered as she hovered. Finally, she said, "I suppose there's a better place to be found, especially if your home is being destroyed. But — and no offense intended, of course — it sounds as if you're scurrying from your home to utopia on a wing and a prayer."

"No offense taken," responded Ms. Ladybug, "and we *are* scurrying on wings, but no prayers."

"And," said Mr. Honeybee, "utopia literally means *no place*. And since we've lost our homes and have nowhere else to go, utopia, or *no place*, seems as good a place as any!"

Slightly taken aback by the intelligence and great knowledge of the ladybug and the honeybee, Lozan looked thoughtfully at the pair. "So, you no longer have a home?"

"That's correct," Ms. Ladybug said. "Our homes have been destroyed. Our tribes," she continued, nodding toward Mr. Honeybee, "similarly have been destroyed."

"There is no reason to stay," added Mr. Honeybee. "There is no home left for us. As nearly as we can determine, we are the last of our kind."

"But maybe there are others," said Ms. Ladybug. "We're trying to find out. We're trying to find a place to live in peace."

Spontaneously, Mr. Honeybee added after a pause, "and you're welcome to join our search."

"If you desire, of course," Ms. Ladybug added. "We welcome anybody who wants to join us."

"Well, not anybody," said Mr. Honeybee. "We only want those who'll try to get along. We only want those who seek the path of peace. We only want those who'll give instead of always just take. Not to put too fine a point on the issue, but we've had enough exposure to 'takers' and hatred and war. We're tired of the never-ending death race. We want to live. And we want to live in harmony. Have a little joy before the end. You know?"

"You seem like my kind of folks," Lozan said slowly. "Mind if I sit a spell?"

"Of course not," said Ms. Ladybug, gesturing toward the nearest branch. "Please join us."

Lozan landed gently on the branch, her wings perpendicular to her body. The blue shine of her translucent wings added to her stunning beauty. "I've had similar issues in my own journey. Loss of family, friends, and home and the like. It does get lonely on the road - when you're the last of your kind." Her large, blue-green eyes became wistful at some passing thought. "I'd like to join you," she said suddenly. "What's your plan? How may I help you?"

Mr. Honeybee and Ms. Ladybug looked at each other, their faces beaming with smiles.

"Lozan, the Last Dragonfly."

CHASING THE NIGHT

Joined by their new companion, the unlikely pair followed the lead of the fireflies into another long night of flight for the third night in a row. Although their budding friendship with Lozan energized all three of them, they struggled as they flew up and over the tree-covered ridge-tops and then down into verdant valleys now starkly lit by the silvery light of the nearly full moon.

The dynamic duo was still unfamiliar with the evening, their senses having evolved over eons to function during the daytime. They had to place an immense amount of trust in the fireflies. Fortunately the sprinkle of fireflies was accustomed to the night and its dangers as well as its beauty and mystery. Mr. Honeybee, Ms. Ladybug, and Lozan struggled again to keep pace, and also struggled to focus on the flickering, blinking fluorescent lights of the fireflies.

The night was humid and warm, and the air around them felt thick, heavy, and oppressive. Mr. Honeybee kept close watch on Ms. Ladybug to make sure she didn't get left behind. Unbeknownst to him, she was doing the same thing. In the short time they had known each other the two had developed a deep and caring friendship that left them feeling protective of the other. Their personal tragedies of loss had brought them together and cemented their friendship with an intimate understanding of the pain each one was experiencing. Neither one could now imagine losing the other. As a result, they looked over their shoulders every few moments to make sure their partner was still there, still with them, still okay.

As they flew behind the fireflies, they were suddenly interrupted by a question: "Why do you keep doing that?" It was Lozan, momentarily forgotten by Mr. Honeybee and Ms. Ladybug, flying right next to them, staring at them from a short distance. They were startled out of their intent focus.

"Doing what?" asked Mr. Honeybee.

"You both keep looking over your shoulders at each other. Why?"

Mr. Honeybee and Ms. Ladybug stared blankly at the blue-and-yellow dragonfly, her colors nearly black in the darkness. The two glanced at each other quickly, and then back at the dragonfly as she continued to stare curiously at them. Lozan flew beside the pair in liquid-like steadiness, her four wings keeping her balanced in flight.

"I don't know," said Mr. Honeybee and Ms. Ladybug simultaneously as they looked at each other, and then back at Lozan.

"I didn't even know I was doing it," said Mr. Honeybee.

"Me, neither," said Ms. Ladybug. "But now that you mention it, I guess I've been keeping an eye on Mr. Honeybee."

"We've become friends, I suppose," replied Mr. Honeybee. "I worry about Ms. Ladybug. And we've had a few incidents. I feel protect ..."

At the moment, a swirling cloud of darkness encircled them. Ms. Ladybug shrieked as she was plucked from the air and into the mouth of a bat. She was immediately overwhelmed by the pungent smell, which reminded her of the fog sprayed by the humans. It was hot and wet and the bat's tongue was coarse. She battled with all her strength to stay in front of the bat's mouth. She knew she'd die if she slid down his throat into his stomach.

"No!" screamed Mr. Honeybee, flying toward the bat. Lozan, too, flew into the swirling matrix of bats. She and Mr.

Honeybee arrived together. Lozan chomped onto the bat's left eye as Mr. Honeybee bit, as hard as his little jaws allowed, onto the bat's right eyelid. The fireflies heard the airborne kerfuffle and circled back to investigate. Seeing Mr. Honeybee and Lozan attached firmly to the bat, they converged as a swarm in the face of the flying mammal.

The bat, stunned by the two-pronged attack on his pained eyes and confused by the sudden swirl of lights, swerved and inadvertently crashed into another bat. Lozan nearly lost her grip on the bat and scrambled to hold on. The bat coughed, and Ms. Ladybug found herself hurtling through the dark night.

Ms. Ladybug tumbled only for a second before righting herself. Seeing the guilty bat above her, with Mr. Honeybee and Lozan attached, she yelled, "I'm free! Down here, guys!"

The honeybee and the dragonfly unleashed their locked jaws from the bat and flew down to meet the ladybug. The fireflies joined the threesome in a flurry of blinking lights. They all continued along their prior route and the bats disappeared into the darkness to search for less quarrelsome prey.

Mr. Honeybee flew close to Ms. Ladybug and asked, "Are you hurt? Are you okay?"

Ms. Ladybug shook the saliva off her wings and performed a couple in-air acrobatic maneuvers. "All systems go," she said.

Mr. Honeybee turned his attention to Eubuleus and the other fireflies as he asked, "Are we safe?"

Eubuleus blinked a few times in rapid succession, took a quick look at the other fireflies, and said, "For now, yes. They desire mosquitoes, and we taste terrible, so I think we've seen the last of them. But let's stick together and keep moving."

Lozan chimed in, "You don't need to ask me twice. That bat nearly took off one of my wings."

PARADISE LOST?

Despite the arduous night, Ms. Ladybug, Mr. Honeybee, and Lozan were too excited to fall immediately into sleep. Ms. Ladybug looked affectionately at the other two and spoke in a solemn voice. "You saved my life, Lozan and Mr. Honeybee. I can never repay you for what you've done."

"Technically," said Mr. Honeybee, "we didn't save your life. We merely extended it."

Picking up on his cue, Lozan said, "That's right, isn't it? Nobody gets out alive."

"As we've discussed before," said Mr. Honeybee, "birth is lethal. We're all dying, since our first moment on Earth. But," continued the honeybee, "while we're here, we have these precious moments." He looked deeply into Ms. Ladybug's eyes.

"I want to spend my moments with those who care, and those whom I care about."

Ms. Ladybug stared back for several quiet seconds before answering but her little heart thumped in her breast. "Living without you would be unimaginable, Mr. Honeybee." She gazed up into his dark eyes, "We only met a few days ago, yet we've grown so close. Even before you saved my life … er, I mean, *extended* my life," she said, glancing at Lozan and then nodding at Mr. Honeybee, "I realized we have something special between us."

"Very special," said Mr. Honeybee. "I'd sting for you, were I able"

Lozan and Ms. Ladybug looked perplexed. Lozan said, "What do you mean?"

Mr. Honeybee pointed his right foreleg at his lower abdomen. "Some of my friends have stingers right there. But I don't. It's not part of my body. But if I had a stinger, I'd surely use it to protect you."

"I see," said Ms. Ladybug. "These stingers are dangerous?"

"They can be very dangerous," said Mr. Honeybee. "They're poisonous."

"Wow," answered Lozan. "So you can hurt somebody?"

"I can't hurt anybody. Being a male, I don't have a stinger," said Mr. Honeybee. "But some of my hive-mates can kill with their stingers."

"Yikes," said Ms. Ladybug. "Have you known somebody to use their stinger to kill somebody? Have you seen it happen?"

"Oh, yes," answered Mr. Honeybee. "And when it happens, the bee is not able to tell the story of how bravely she defended the hive from the yellow jackets."

Lozan and Ms. Ladybug looked at Mr. Honeybee. Perplexed, Lozan asked, "What do you mean, Mr. Honeybee?"

"Upon using the stinger, it dislodges from the bee's body and the bee dies. Use of the stinger hurts or kills another, but the act kills the bee doing the stinging, too. It's a last resort to protect the hive, to protect our family." He looked down as painful emotions washed over him.

Ms. Ladybug let this information sink in. Initially, she was sad on Mr. Honeybee's behalf. Then she realized the immensity of what he was saying, and she became simultaneously sad and excited. "You would sting for me?"

"Yes, Ms. Ladybug, I would sting for you, if only I were able." Mr. Honeybee continued, "I would die for you."

As he stared into her eyes, now brimming with tears, Mr. Honeybee was overcome with a warm feeling he'd only previously experienced with his queen and happy hive of nieces and nephews. He hadn't thought he'd ever feel this way again, at least not this soon after losing his entire world. The tenderness that welled up in his chest for this black speckled lady startled him and even scared him a little. If he lost Lady, too — and Lady is what he called her in his mind — he wasn't quite sure how or even *why* he'd carry on. She was his last link to something sweet and warm and familiar, and his heart felt as if it would break with the mere thought of losing her. He could only hope that Ms. Ladybug was having very similar thoughts about him at the very same moment as she gazed sweetly into his dark, multifaceted eyes, her own dark eyes sparkling with tears.

In the awkward silence that followed Lozan piped up, "Well, you're gonna die anyway. But what a way to go." The three burst into raucous laughter.

"Yes," Ms. Ladybug said, "Have a drink. Chew some wildwood weed. Throw a party. You're gonna die anyway."

They all giggled at the thought before Lozan answered, "That path is the one that appeals to nearly everybody I know. But I think there's more to life than taking the first train to hedonism."

"So do we," said Ms. Ladybug. "We're trying to awaken everybody to the dangers we face now and the ones looming on the horizon. It would be easier to get on with our own lives and party as if there's no tomorrow."

"But," interrupted Mr. Honeybee, "if everybody does that, we'll ensure there's no tomorrow."

Lozan grew quiet for a moment and Ms. Ladybug noticed. "What are you thinking, Lozan?"

Lozan stared at the spotted beetle and became serious. "I am carrying my tomorrows inside of me, but I am terrified of the world they will be coming into. The dangers they will face."

"Well, I'm certain you will be there for them and do your very best to protect them," Mr. Honeybee said, trying to reassure Lozan.

However, Lozan shook her large-eyed head and her eyes sparkled with tears now. "No I shall not be here for them."

"Whatever do you mean, Lozan? Why would you not be here?" asked Ms. Ladybug with concern in her voice.

"I am already dying." Lozan's voice was small and weak, and filled with fear and sorrow.

"What? But how? We did not travel through any poisons today! I'm certain you're going to be just fine!"

"No, it's not any poison. It's my life span. I've reached the end of it. I lived a long and beautiful life under streams and ponds as a nymph, and now I've transformed and grown wings, found my mate, and now search for the perfect body of water to lay my eggs and then return to the water one last time."

Ms. Ladybug and Mr. Honeybee, stunned by this new information, stared in silence for a long time at Lozan, daughter of Geronimo and Alope, their hearts breaking. Tears rolled down Ms. Ladybug's cheeks and Lozan reached out a long foreleg to gently wipe it away.

"Don't weep for me, Ms. Ladybug. All things must die. Imagine if no one died? Why there'd be no room left for anyone! We'd all be standing on top of each other! We'd look pretty ridiculous, if you ask me. Dying is part of the cycle of life. It makes room for new eyes and ears to see the beautiful world we have lived in." She rubbed her abdomen, "I'm just concerned about my little ones and the world they will be coming into. They won't have the beauty and abundance that we had. And I won't be here to help them or to protect them."

At those words Mr. Honeybee's eyes lit up! Protecting a young brood was something with which he was well acquainted.

"That's where we can help you, Lozan! We have longer lifespans than you, though who knows! With the way things are going, we may well be heading into the abyss at your side. But if we survive until your hatchlings hatch, I swear we will look after them and do our very best to protect them!" He smiled with renewed excitement and a feeling of hope that he had not experienced in a long time. "What do you say Ms. Ladybug? Are you in?"

A huge grin broke across Ms. Ladybug's tear-streaked face and she stood with arms akimbo, cocked her little head, "Do you even have to ask?" She turned her gaze compassionately to Lozan's huge, blue-green eyes.

"Darling Lozan, Mr. Honeybee is a genius. He and I would be proud to be foster parents to your little nymphs. Even if we cannot be under water with them, we will do our best to protect them and give them some guidance so that they know what lies ahead."

Lozan burst into tears and hugged Ms. Ladybug and Mr. Honeybee at the same time. She trembled with emotion and great relief.

"Oh my dear friends, you have no idea how happy you've just made me," although her sobbing seemed to indicate otherwise. "I'm the happiest dragonfly about to die! And all thanks to your willingness to help. And for nothing in return!" She sniffled and thought about it some more. "I've known a few like you. Like us. I don't know why some of us are committed to service, but most are not. I don't know why the party rages on, with endless participation from the endless, mindless masses, while we stand on the fringe, looking in. There is such a difference between the cycle of life that includes death as a process of transformation, and the culture of death that just kills as a means to an end, for greed."

Ms. Ladybug nodded and added thoughtfully, "Does it mean we're weird, talking about dying?"

"It does seem weird," said Mr. Honeybee. "Either there's something wrong with us, or there's something wrong with everybody else."

"There's certainly something wrong," Lozan said. "A culture of death cannot continue forever." She rubbed her abdomen thoughtfully. There was some hope, though not much, for her little ones. It was hard not to think of hope, despite the earlier conversation. She was warmed by the excitement that her two companions expressed as they volunteered to help her and her progeny. Perhaps the project of looking out for her little ones gave them hope, too. Well, maybe not hope so much, but a purpose. Yes, that was it. They had a reason for living again, one that went beyond themselves. Purposeful living, and being present were the keys, rather than being lost in sad memories or living in fear of tomorrow. It was action that gave her hope, not hope that created the action.

"This death cult that most humans are embedded within seems to be working fine so far," answered Mr. Honeybee in a somber tone. "And it seems like forever."

"Which is a long time," said Ms. Ladybug in a chirpy, uplifting tone, "especially toward the end."

"If you think forever has an end, then I don't think you understand forever," said Mr. Honeybee, his mood improved by Ms. Ladybug's joke.

"And there's a big difference between mostly forever and completely forever," said Lozan. "With mostly forever, there's still a chance to change the outcome. With completely forever, we're all dead."

"But we're all dead anyway," said Ms. Ladybug.

"Eventually," said Mr. Honeybee.

"Everyone knows that everyone dies. But not tonight," Lozan said. "Tonight we live. Tonight we embrace each moment, with each other." Tonight, she thought silently, we are present and accounted for. She was contented with the thought.

"Tonight we live," reflected Ms. Ladybug, "and tomorrow, too. And every day, until we don't. Until we can't. Until the abyss calls to us."

Lozan yawned heartily and said, "The abyss is calling me right now. I hope it's temporary. Sleepy-time for me."

"Me, too," echoed Ms. Ladybug.

"Until tomorrow, then, my friends," said Mr. Honeybee resolutely. His tummy growled again and ignoring it he snuggled closer to his sweetie, Lady.

SEEKING PARADISE

The next evening, Mr. Honeybee, Ms. Ladybug, and Lozan arose again earlier than the fireflies. They stretched themselves awake and were finally starting to feel energetic after sleeping during the day. Mr. Honeybee had found a windfall of food, a cracked and overturned maple syrup canister on the side of a road. It was being quickly collected by all manner of nectar-eating bugs, wasps and ants, but they made room for the little bee who looked a little too hungry to go on much further. By the time they took to the air at the end of the day, they were able to keep pace with the fireflies and Mr. Honeybee had plenty of energy for a change.

It seemed that they had flown for several hours and just as the threesome felt as if their strength was about to wane again, the full moon reached its zenith in the night sky, and the fireflies slowed and then stopped. They hovered near a small stream and engaged in a flurry of blinking. Finally Eubuleus turned to Mr. Honeybee, Ms. Ladybug, and Lozan. "We think this is the place we've been seeking."

Ms. Ladybug and Mr. Honeybee looked around and could distinguish nothing special about this place. They looked at each other with obvious curiosity. They wanted to believe the fireflies and they didn't want to question their authority, but they were skeptical.

Using the most polite tone she could muster, Ms. Ladybug said, "Here? Why here?"

"It's difficult for you to see at night," answered Eubuleus, "but this place is quite unusual. It's an oasis of wildness in an ocean of humans and their impacts. Apparently the humans set it aside as some sort of reserve for the rest of us. They call it a national park."

Mr. Honeybee tentatively answered, "It seems nice enough. I guess we'll know more in the morning."

Eubuleus continued, "Quite recently it's been given the customary human treatment. Nasty humans, anyway. They found those materials that allow them go faster: coal, oil, gas. So they began their customary destructive ways. But that started only recently. Before that, it was a very large area mostly undisturbed by humans."

Ms. Ladybug said, "Shall we settle down, then? We can take a close look when the sun rises."

Lozan broke in by saying, "Excuse me! My situation is becoming urgent. I need to find a place for my eggs. Immediately! Will you help?" She looked directly at Ms. Ladybug as she spoke.

"Yes, of course," said Ms. Ladybug. "How can we help? And where?"

Lozan nodded her head toward a stand of tall vegetation where the water was still and answered, "Over there." And she hastily flew away in that direction, counting on the others to follow.

And the others did follow, right behind the beautiful, but suddenly distressed dragonfly.

Several times, Lozan hovered above a spot, and then moved a short distance further. Finally she landed a few inches above the water on a tall bit of cattail. She looked closely down at the water as Mr. Honeybee, Ms. Ladybug, and the fireflies rested on various bits of vegetation. The water rippled beneath Lozan like liquid silver reflecting the full moon, and the sounds of frogs and crickets filled the cool, night air. Far in the distance the sound of coyotes yipping cut through the night.

"This looks like the spot," Lozan said to nobody in particular. "I need to lay my eggs on that bit of submerged vegetation, just below the surface of the water."

Lozan landed softly on the water and tucked her abdomen beneath the water. Her eggs immediately began to come out her abdomen. They stuck to the bit of vegetation below the surface of the water. Lozan smiled as a faraway look appeared in her eyes. "My darlings will have a future here."

Everybody else was respectfully silent. They marveled at the glorious process as life gave way to new life.

In a few moments, Lozan was done. She looked up at the unlikely spectators above her and smiled broadly. "That's all, folks! The show's over."

Ms. Ladybug asked, "Lozan, what shall we do?"

Lozan flew a short distance and landed a few inches above the water before answering. "Just keep an eye on them for a few days or weeks. After that, they'll assume a different form. They'll turn into nymphs. Then they're on their own. Some will be eaten by frogs and fish. Some won't live long, but there's not much you can do about that."

They all looked around, making eye contact and feeling uplifted by Lozan's trust in them. The fireflies stopped blinking and quietly rested on the vegetation, their bodies shining in the light of the eternal satellite, Seline.

"Thank you," said Ms. Ladybug. "Thank you for sharing this beautiful moment with us, and for trusting us with your offspring."

Lozan looked closely at Ms. Ladybug, and then at Mr. Honeybee. Softly, she said, "You're my friends. Of course I trust you." She looked back down into the water to check on the freshly laid eggs. She could just make out their pale orbs clustered there upon a submerged leaf. She smiled at them with a motherly smile. They would never know the sound of her wings, or the gaze of her blue eyes, or how their father bravely sacrificed himself for them. *My beautiful Cochise, we did it. Wait for me on the other side.*

Ms. Ladybug and Mr. Honeybee chatted back and forth a bit, basking in the glow of their trusted friendship with Lozan. During the brief conversation, they failed to notice that Lozan was struggling to hang onto the cattail, her wings askew from their normal resting position. She attracted their attention with a raspy cough.

"Oh, Lozan," asked Ms. Ladybug in a concerned tone, "are you okay?"

"Well, yes and no," said Lozan, to bemused looks all around. "You see, my kind usually dies shortly after giving birth. I spent most of my life in other, smaller forms: eggs first, and especially nymphs. The 'adult' version of me wears out darned quickly. And it looks like my time is up and I will soon be joining my father, Geronimo and mother Alope and the father of my children, Cochise."

Ms. Ladybug and Mr. Honeybee glanced at each other, and then turned their eyes back on Lozan. Mr. Honeybee said, "What can we do? How can we help?"

Lozan paused thoughtfully, her strength fading before their attentive eyes. "There's nothing to be done, really. In an ideal world I would have many of my kind with me as I die. But — and stop me if you've noticed this one," she said wryly — "this is hardly an ideal world."

"Well, we're not going to simply let you die," said Mr. Honeybee. "There must be something we can do." He looked around helplessly, his eyes begging for a response from Ms. Ladybug. She simply looked silently back at him.

"As you know, Mr. Honeybee," said Lozan, "life is a gift. But it doesn't last forever."

"Acceptance is a gift, too," said Ms. Ladybug in a gentle tone. "Accepting the brevity of our time in this realm helps us to appreciate the moments we have."

"And make them better," responded Mr. Honeybee, finally coming to grips with Lozan's demise. The recent conversations he'd had with Ms. Ladybug came rushing to the fore. Life is short. Nobody gets out alive. Live as though the moments are what we have. Create moments of joy and beauty. Be here now! Ms. Ladybug was remembering, too. She and Mr. Honeybee had shared several adventures during their emotional journey. And yet, a thought was nagging at her, emerging from beneath the memories. It took her a minute to articulate the thought. "We're always told to plan for tomorrow. We're encouraged to deny our own death. It's no wonder we have such a hard time when our friends die."

Lozan was fading quickly. She could barely keep her head up. Mr. Honeybee and Ms. Ladybug were shocked into inaction. Despite having watched their own families and friends in their tribes die and be wiped out completely, it was never easy to see death so close at hand, and so suddenly. It always felt like the first time. Finally, Ms. Ladybug had an idea: "We have to make this easy for Lozan. It's not about us. Mr. Honeybee, will you join me in hugging Lozan?"

"Of course," replied Mr. Honeybee, and he joined Ms. Ladybug in stepping toward Lozan. Awkwardly, they put their tiny legs on Lozan's body.

Eubuleus blinked fervently as he looked at the sprinkling of fireflies. They all blinked chaotically and then moved to within a few inches of Lozan, all landing on vegetation in front of her. Once settled in place, they blinked in unison, one second "on" and then two seconds "off."

The three friends were washed in the soft golden-green glow of hundreds of fireflies encircling them. Among them the celestial queen of the night hung from a thin thread, silvery and shimmering in the evening haze. The night had grown silent, the sense of dark expectation heavy in the air.

Ms. Ladybug said, "Thank you, Lozan, for coming into my life. You not only extended my life when the bat tried to eat me for supper. You also enriched my life. You are a wise and wonderful friend. I will always remember."

Lozan merely shook her tired head. She was unable to speak.

Mr. Honeybee said, "You're the first one I've known beyond my kind." He paused and added, "Well, except for Ms. Ladybug, of course." His eyes met those of Ms. Ladybug, and he touched her foreleg gently with his own. "I am so glad we met, Lozan. You taught me how to live. You showed me how to live with ferocity ... with commitment ... with passion ... and with love, instead of with fear."

Lozan smiled as her head dropped. Her front left wing fluttered once. Then she was still.

Ms. Ladybug and Mr. Honeybee immediately burst into tears. Sobbing, Ms. Ladybug said, "She's gone." The two friends embraced tearfully, sharing their sorrow.

The fireflies went dark. Eubuleus shed a single tear and was surrounded by other slightly younger elders. Ms. Ladybug and Mr. Honeybee, heartbroken at the death of Lozan, cried themselves to sleep inside a little knothole in a Cottonwood tree overlooking the shallow pond. The dragonfly had become a wonderful friend in very little time.

Awakening

Still somber as they arose the next morning, Ms. Ladybug and Mr. Honeybee did not speak for a long time. The fireflies were still sleeping and the body of Lozan, still fresh in their minds, was floating in the water near her eggs.

After a long time without words between them, Ms. Ladybug said, "I've spent a long time with some of my own kind and never become close to them. But we knew Lozan only briefly and yet we love her."

"*Loved* her," said Mr. Honeybee. "She's gone, Ms. Ladybug."

Ms. Ladybug burst into tears. "I know. But it's so hard. She was just right here a moment ago."

"I know it's a cliché," said Mr. Honeybee, "but it's the moments that matter. Lozan became our friend almost immediately. Why is that?"

"Oh, Mr. Honeybee, you have to come up with a formula for everything, don't you?"

Intent upon determining a solution, Mr. Honeybee ignored Ms. Ladybug's comment. "I think it's periods of stress. The quality of the moment is important: more important, even, than the quantity of them."

Ms. Ladybug sighed and gave into Mr. Honeybee's analytical approach. "We went into battle together. She risked her life to save mine." After a short pause and a quick glance at Mr. Honeybee, she said, "I mean, to extend my life."

Mr. Honeybee nodded his head in agreement and said, "Right. I think it's those tests." He was fumbling to find the right words. "Those moments that test us, I mean. Those are the moments that bring us together."

"Emotional moments," said Ms. Ladybug. "We get closer to each other by sharing moments of danger, and also moments of grief." She looked up into his eyes as she said, "And moments of joy." He noticed her intention and reached out to hug her.

He murmured into her shoulder, "Yes, joy brings us together too."

After a moment's silence Mr. Honeybee said, "I think judgment is important, too. When others judge us harshly because of our emotions, that's no help at all. That kind of behavior pushes us apart."

Ms. Ladybug thought long and hard before responding. "We must accept our differences instead of judging our differences. I think that's the biggest part of the story."

"Just as we've accepted each other," said Mr. Honeybee. "So, too, must everybody else, if we are to persist into the future. Seeing others as inferior isn't working."

"But it's what these humans do best," said Ms. Ladybug. "They believe they're superior. They also believe they don't need the rest of us, so they kill us with their every cultural act. However, in killing us all, they are also killing themselves."

"They don't seem to be able to help it."

"Of course not," said Ms. Ladybug. "They've been doing it so long, they don't know any other way. They believe it's the only way. And the few who resist are crushed, so the whole disastrous system keeps moving in the same horrible direction."

"And it's not as if many are willing to resist," said Mr. Honeybee. "Resisting the cultural current of the main stream is nearly impossible. The ideas underlying the system are riddled with lies, but the lies are too persuasive to resist."

"Everybody wants more and better," said Ms. Ladybug. "Everyone wants infinite growth on a finite planet, and with no adverse consequences."

"The equation doesn't make any sense," said Mr. Honeybee, the frustration evident in his voice.

"But if a lie is repeated often enough, and it's a lie you want to hear, maybe you can no longer tell it's a lie. Maybe you want to believe it so badly, that you just start believing it. It's easier to believe the lie — the lie everybody else believes — than to constantly seek the truth."

"Right," said Mr. Honeybee. "If you're the only one looking for the truth, you'll be viewed as crazy. You won't fit into the culture of fantasy."

"And the further a society drifts from the truth, the less likely the truth-seeker will be accepted by the society."

"Much less the teller of truths," said Mr. Honeybee. "The lies are more comfortable than the facts, so the facts are denied. When the entire set of living arrangements is based on lies, there's no way to spread the truth."

Mr. Honeybee said, "It's not even that the facts are denied. They just aren't part of the conversation."

"I guess that's right," answered Ms. Ladybug after a short, thoughtful pause. "If you don't even know enough to ask relevant questions, you're never going to find the answers."

"And most of the entire human culture, as least what I've observed, is focused on minor, nonsensical distractions. There's no time for a serious conversation because the humans are captivated by the noisy, artificial lenses attached to the walls of their caves."

"Sometimes," chimed in Ms. Ladybug, "they go outside. But mostly to watch their warriors engage in contests."

"It's funny," answered Mr. Honeybee. "They don't even know the people who are committing terrible acts of violence, but they respect and love them more than they love their own families. And the warriors don't return their respect or love."

Ms. Ladybug blinked in amazement. "Wow. I guess that's right, isn't it?"

Mr. Honeybee said, "It's a culture of celebrity worship. It's a culture of spectacle. And it's all illusory."

"It seems real to them," said Ms. Ladybug. "You have to pity the fools."

"But the whole thing is hero worship based on a rock-solid foundation of lies. It has nothing to do with anything meaningful. It's not based on water, or food, or any other elements of survival. It's not based on love. Rather, it's based on fear. They work so hard to find meaning in their lives, but they're looking in all the wrong places."

"They need to look at themselves, not at their heroes," said Ms. Ladybug. "They ought to be looking inside, but instead they're looking for an easy answer beyond themselves."

"Well," said Mr. Honeybee with a smile, "it seems we solved all their problems. And, by extension, we've solved all our problems, too."

"I don't think the humans heard us this time any better than at our Morse code attempt. And I doubt they'd follow our advice anyway," Ms. Ladybug groused. "It all seems so pointless."

Mr. Honeybee paused thoughtfully. "I suppose it *is* pointless, beyond us and our limited understanding. But I still want to know what's happening in the world, even if we cannot solve all our problems. Maybe we can't solve any of them."

"I agree," said Ms. Ladybug. "I'd rather know the truth than live the lie."

Mr. Honeybee smiled even more broadly as he said, "We'd make terrible humans."

"Yes," responded Ms. Ladybug. "It seems they'd rather be incurious humans than enlightened insects."

"I don't think they have a choice," said Mr. Honeybee.

"And," answered Ms. Ladybug, "neither do we. After all, we didn't get to decide when and where to show up. We just popped into the world without being asked."

"It's the same for the humans. Do you suppose they'd even be here, if they had the choice?"

"I don't think they think about it. Indeed," continued Ms. Ladybug, "I don't think they think about much of anything."

"Ergo, their incuriosity," said Mr. Honeybee still holding onto Ms. Ladybug, even after the long intellectual conversation spoken mostly into her shiny, tiny shoulder.

"Not to change the subject," said Ms. Ladybug into his broad, golden and furry chest, "but I guess we'd better look around. We need to determine if this place is all it's cracked up to be."

Mr. Honeybee sighed regretfully, still clutching her tightly, "But I was just starting to enjoy myself." She chuckled softly into his chest and squeezed him a little tighter and he gasped with surprise. They laughed together and slowly pulled apart, still holding onto their forelimbs, smiling into each other's eyes.

PARADISE FOUND?

As it turned out, the place was good. It wasn't great, like the places they used to know. But those days were long gone. This place had bogs and rivers and lakes filled with fish and frogs and water skippers. It had hillsides covered with gold and blue flowers and valleys filled with myriad grasses bordering meandering streams. It had rabbits and deer and blue skies. It had deep, loamy soils with dozens of species — no, hundreds — in the upper few inches.

They breathed deep. The air was clear, clean, and sweet.

They drank the water from a stream. It was clear, clean, and sweet.

They were giddy with excitement. This place seemed like the real deal.

"Wow," said Mr. Honeybee, "not bad, eh?"

"Not bad at all," said Ms. Ladybug. "I could get used to this."

Mr. Honeybee landed upon a small yellow flower and inhaled a big sniff. "This is a great place to stop and smell the flowers."

"Not only that," she said, "but it's a great place to *keep* smelling the flowers. It's a great place to settle down."

Mr. Honeybee said, "The trouble is, you think there's time."

Ms. Ladybug responded, "The trouble is, you think there's not."

Mr. Honeybee said, "My quote is from a wise man many centuries ago."

"Mine is contemporary. It's from me, just now. It works for today."

He was taken aback by her. She was so clever! He had thought he knew everything, but no! She was wise beyond her years and he enjoyed hearing every word that came out of her mouth. He appreciated how she communicated with him and with others. She listened to what other bugs had to say and was thoughtful and kind, but also unafraid of speaking her mind and completely unafraid of taking control of a situation! She was as independent and in control as his beautiful queen had been, and yet she was willing to share responsibility with those around her. He watched her as she surveyed the area from atop a daisy that hung over the little inlet pond where Lozan had laid her eggs. Lady caught him staring at her and broke into a huge grin and waved her tiny arm. He waved back and felt happy and smiled broadly.

Ms. Ladybug, sitting upon a white daisy, was filled with a mixture of emotions that left her feeling as if she might explode. Her little beetle heart could only take so many different feelings before it burst. Foremost she was feeling grief-stricken at the loss of a friend. The sorrow would well up through her belly and past her heart, up her throat and into her eyes until it spilled out in the form of tears that seemed to have no end. Alternately, she was also feeling joyful! Every moment she shared with Mr. Honeybee was a total pleasure, and lifted her up off her six little feet and into the air. Every glance and every smile he gave her made her heart fill with excitement and happiness that she had never felt before. And he was so clever! Not to mention handsome. For a bee, that is. She had never before been attracted to a bee and she was surprised at herself. Her kind and his kind always kept to themselves, there was never any interaction save a polite "excuse me" upon a flower, let alone a deep friendship or an emotional relationship! Her thought startled her. *An emotional relationship? Is that what is happening?*

She glanced at Honey, for that is what she called him in her thoughts. He was busy devouring nectar from a bachelor button flower and looked quite content with his work. Near him were a few bumblebees busily foraging, but no other European honeybees except Mr. Honeybee. She felt a pang of sorrow for him, imagining the loneliness he must feel at having lost his entire hive and perhaps his entire species.

He would sting for me, if he could! She recalled his words and felt a surge of excitement again, and felt very protective of him. *And if I had a stinger I would sting for him too! I know I would!* However, she had no scary stinger or poison, or anything dangerous to fight with. All she had was a strong mandible that could chew up an aphid or pollen for a meal, which was exactly what she was doing at the present moment. Suddenly she felt very small and very fragile and very impotent. Ms. Ladybug looked around at the beautiful place the fireflies had found for them, and she sighed.

I guess I must content myself with who and what I am. It's not so bad after all. I suppose we all have our gifts. Some of us seem to have more gifts than others. She watched the handsome honeybee darting nimbly between the myriad flowers, tasting and testing, choosing what he was in the mood for, and just at that moment he glanced up again and this time it was his turn to catch her staring his way. Her little heart fluttered as he broke into a huge grin and did a happy somersault for her in mid-air.

Then he pantomimed going down an escalator behind a flower and then back up an escalator behind another flower. She laughed at his antics and clapped her tiny forelimb hands as he carried on with the little show. Mr. Honeybee was thrilled that he could make her laugh and pulled out all the stops for her. Using a bachelor button flower as a hat and a honeysuckle stem as a cane, he did a little vaudeville dance in mid-air for her that knocked her laughing off of her daisy. Horrified that she fell, he dashed to her side and caught her in the air still giggling her little head off.

"Oh Mr. Honeybee, you are hilarious! I so needed a good laugh!"

He grinned broadly and floated her back up to her flower where he gently set her back down. Then he bowed gallantly to her, and she fluttered her eyes and curtseyed to him. Above them a hermit thrush began singing his morning song and Mr. Honeybee got an idea.

He asked, lifting his forelimb to her, "May I have this dance?"

Ms. Ladybug smiled softly and placed her tiny forelimb in his. "Yes, please."

He pulled her into him, tight into him, and she sighed as his many arms held her close and lifted them both up and off the flower. Light as the wind, they twirled above the flowers as the hermit thrush sang his semi-mournful song that echoed in the tiny valley. She felt as if she had found a small patch of paradise and rested her head against his shoulder. A tear coursed its way down her cheek and, as he noticed in mid-spiral, he gazed down into her face.

"It's going to be okay, Ms. Ladybug."

She smiled sadly up at him, "No it's not, but that's okay. I found you. I found you at the end of time."

His heart exploded with joy at her words.

"We found each other. And you saved me, Ms. Ladybug."

"We saved each other," she said, still smiling her sweet, sad smile.

"You always have to have the last word don't you?" He teased.

"Mmmmmmyes!" She laughed, and he twirled her higher and held her tighter and she loved every moment of it.

TROUBLE IN PARADISE

As they twirled together, Mr. Honeybee suddenly smelled smoke. Like others of his kind, he was keenly equipped to smell smoke. Startled and worried, he said, "I smell smoke, Ms. Ladybug. There's a fire nearby."

She sniffed, but could smell nothing unusual. "Are you sure?"

"I'm sure," he said. "We need to get out of here." He was excited, and was becoming agitated at Ms. Ladybug's lackadaisical attitude.

"What about the eggs? We promised Lozan we'd watch over them."

"They're under water," he assured her. "They'll be safe. But if there's a fire coming, we must seek refuge. The heat will kill us."

"But," she said.

"No buts," Mr. Honeybee broke in. "I feel terribly guilty about leaving Lozan's body, and her eggs. But I don't think she'd want us to die as a result of our concern. She's already dead, Ms. Ladybug, and her eggs will be fine."

Ms. Ladybug hesitated, still unsure about leaving the eggs. They'd made a promise.

As if he were reading her mind, Mr. Honeybee said, "I know we promised Lozan we'd take care of the eggs. But we can't watch over them if we're dead. We'll come back to check the eggs as soon as it's safe."

She asked, "Promise?"

"Yes," he said. "I promise."

"Okay," she said, "let's find Eubuleus and the fireflies." For the first time, real fear tinged her voice.

"I think they're still sleeping. Probably over there," said Mr. Honeybee, pointing with his right foreleg as he flew in the direction he pointed.

The fireflies quickly sprang to attention and they all followed Mr. Honeybee's lead. His excellent sense of smell indicated the origin of the smoke, and they flew the opposite direction. They were on their way within a few seconds.

They were not alone. The air was filled with birds, and they saw deer running below them. The air was turbulent, and their tiny bodies were buffeted by the irregular winds. Within minutes, wisps of smoke accompanied them.

A bluebird flew into their tight swarm and tried to pluck Mr. Honeybee out of the air. Fortunately, a thermal elevated the insects and the bird barely missed its target.

"Whoa, Mr. Honeybee," yelled Ms. Ladybug, "that was a close call."

"Everybody's got to eat," he hollered back at her with a grin.

"They don't need to eat *you*," she said, worry obvious in her voice.

Suddenly they were surrounded by dozens of flying cockroaches. With their large bodies, the roaches were faster and more stable in the air than the smaller insects.

One of the cockroaches asked in a raspy voice, "Care for a ride?"

"What do you mean?" said Ms. Ladybug.

"We're all going the same direction, but we're stronger and faster than you. No offense intended, of course. The birds don't much care to eat us, either. You can hop a ride on our backs."

"Really? You'd do that for us?"

"Come on aboard!"

And they did. Mr. Honeybee climbed aboard one roach while Ms. Ladybug landed safely on another. The fireflies joined in, too, with two of them on the back of each roach.

"Now we're sailing," said Mr. Honeybee excitedly.

"Wheeeeeeeee," replied Ms. Ladybug.

They flew and they flew and they flew. The roaches seemed tireless despite the frequent thermal updrafts and often-changing speed and direction of the wind. Ms. Ladybug, Mr. Honeybee, and the fireflies hung on silently, seemingly for hours.

Eventually it was clear they'd flown beyond danger. They could no longer smell smoke, and the ever-changing wind settled into a relatively constant, light breeze. No longer afraid, they found refuge in a high-mountain meadow filled with green grass and flowers of every color. They were all exhausted from the rapid flight and the excitement of their escape.

After a few words of thanks from the smaller insects to the roaches, they all rested for several hours. Very little was said among them. As nightfall approached, the fireflies began to flutter about. Initially there were only a couple of them, but soon they were all performing a glowing dance a few feet above ground.

One of the roaches was first to speak. He turned to Ms. Ladybug and said, "We'll go back in the morning."

She asked, "So soon?"

"We've seen many of these fires. It's safe to return in a few hours. And, for us, it's home."

Ms. Ladybug and Mr. Honeybee looked at each other. Still tired and traumatized from their days-long adventure, they were feeling indecisive.

Mr. Honeybee finally spoke, albeit wearily. "What do you want to do, Ms. Ladybug? Shall we return?"

Ms. Ladybug said, "Yes. We need to check on Lozan's eggs. And I trust the roaches."

"As you wish, Ms. Ladybug," said Mr. Honeybee.

Ms. Ladybug smiled before she said, "Tomorrow, then. Tomorrow we go back to Lozan's legacy."

Mr. Honeybee sighed and said, "We'd better get some sleep tonight. We have a long journey ahead of us."

EVER AFTER

The area they'd fled a day earlier was barely recognizable. The fire had burned much of the vegetation, although some areas were completely untouched. The patchy mosaic of burned and unburned areas was confusing compared to the many shades of green they'd left behind only a day before.

They located the still waters harboring Lozan's eggs. The stream bank was scorched black, and even the cattails were singed. The eggs appeared unharmed by the fire, and the water was clear and cool. Mr. Honeybee and Ms. Ladybug hovered above the eggs for a close look.

"I think they're going to make it," said the happy Ms. Ladybug.

"And the water is clean," said Mr. Honeybee, obviously relieved.

"We did all right," said Ms. Ladybug, looking affectionately at Mr. Honeybee.

"We're not a bad team."

"That, sir, is an understatement of magnificent proportions," said Ms. Ladybug. "We're an awesome team."

They spent the rest of the afternoon and evening frolicking near Lozan's eggs. They checked the eggs every few minutes, worrying over them as if they were their own. They found food in the unburned patches of vegetation and saw insects and other animals of all kinds. Beyond the occasional friendly greeting, they didn't interact with the others. They were busily enjoying themselves and watching over the eggs.

Each day was filled with places to explore, and new discoveries. Mr. Honeybee and Ms. Ladybug scarcely believed the wonder of the valley to which the fireflies had brought them. Mr. Honeybee had even managed to befriend a couple bumblebees and had scored a daily sip of honey in return for the same dance routine he'd given Ms. Ladybug the first day they'd arrived. Apparently Ms. Ladybug hadn't been the only one amused by his theatrics and he'd garnered a bit of a reputation for being an entertainer. His reputation for hilarity was growing. Before they even realized it, a week had gone by and it was time for Lozan's eggs to hatch. Ms. Ladybug was all in a tizzy over the imminent birth of the naiads and had set up a mini campsite next to the eggs in anticipation of the great event.

A tiny lean-to made of twigs and leaves that had survived the fire sheltered her from the hot sun. As Ms. Ladybug intently watched the eggs under the water, she sipped a little water from a huge dewdrop on a flower petal that Mr. Honeybee had left her. He'd been out foraging most of the day, since he required more food than she did, and was just now arriving with his forelegs clutching a drop of honey the bumblebees had just shared with him. He was saving it to share with Ms. Ladybug. It was a daily ritual that he very much enjoyed.

"Ms. Ladybug! Anything yet?" He asked as he joined her in her little lean-to.

"No, but I expect things to start happening very soon. The eggs are all a quiver and rolling every which way!" He held his treat before her and her eyes widened! She sipped with delight and he tucked in to join her as well. Together they sipped the little drop of honey as they watched Lozan's eggs rolling wildly about. Before long, the eggs began to slowly split one at a time, and translucent naiads gradually emerged, slowly pulling themselves out of their safe enclosures. Mr. Honeybee and Ms. Ladybug cheered them on as excitedly as humans cheered athletes. They whooped and hollered each time a naiad completed his or her exit, and they were beginning to attract some attention. Curious insects passing by, along with other small animals, had heard the commotion and approached to see what was going on. What they saw was a little honeybee and a tiny ladybug hollering and jumping up and down on a leaf that hung over the pond. They could not see the naiads hatching under the water.

A bumblebee with her friend was watching the two bouncing up and down, and she commented to her friend, "They must be practicing for a new show." Her friend nodded in agreement. "He's much better than her," they both agreed heartily.

Once all the hatchlings were free of their confines, Ms. Ladybug announced it was time for her and Mr. Honeybee to introduce themselves and to let the naiads know who their mother was. But it would not be easy because they would have to talk into the water and that would take some clever acrobatics and breath-holding. Amazingly, they managed to accomplish this extraordinary and never-been-done-before feat by having Mr. Honeybee clutch Ms. Ladybug's back legs and hold her suspended over the water. He would dip her just low enough for her to put her face into the water and speak. Her voice was bubbly under water and it made her giggle, a sound that caught the naiads' attention right away. The translucent naiads listened intently to the ladybug and the bee as they explained who they were and what their purpose was.

"We are daughters and sons of Lozan, daughter of Geronimo and Alope. Our father was Cochise who died to protect our mother and us." They chirped in their underwater choir. And Ms. Ladybug and Mr. Honeybee glowed with pride as if Lozan's children were their own. They warned the naiads about the state of the world and told them to enjoy their underwater world and not be thinking too much about when they were going to be grownups. The naiads were indeed grateful and also wise, despite having just been born. Ms. Ladybug chalked that up to them being a 300,000,000-year-old species that predated dinosaurs. They wouldn't have made it this long on Earth if they'd been a selfish, over breeding and unwise species!

Finally, completely exhausted as the sun was setting, Ms. Ladybug and Mr. Honeybee decided to sit in their favorite tree and watch over their little family as the sun completed its scarlet and golden descent. Crickets began to announce the coming of night, and the deep, tremulous sound of a bullfrog surprised the otherwise quiet dusk. Somewhere in the distance, a wolf howled and was answered by another and soon the night was full of the lonesome song of the wolves crying to the crescent moon.

The bee and the ladybug sat quietly next to each other in a partially scorched cottonwood tree as the night grew dark. The moon climbed the horizon in the east. Below them in the pond they could just make out the phosphorescent bodies of Lozan's nymphs as they swam about searching for food.

Ms. Ladybug leaned into Mr. Honeybee and sighed. "Honey, it's been quite a journey with you."

He shot her a glance, his eyes passionate and filled with love. "Lady, you ain't just kiddin'." In a flash he kissed his sweetheart under the silvery moon. Hundreds of fireflies swirled about their heads, spiraling up toward the moonlight where the last of the world's lunar moths fluttered about, seeking sweethearts of their own. Because in the end, only love remains.

PAULINE SCHNEIDER was born in Nigeria and has lived on three continents. She was raised in Greece until the age of 15. She now lives in Westchester County, New York with her 7 pets and youngest daughter. She has been drawing and writing since childhood, holds three degrees including a Master of Education, and recently completed her first documentary, *Going Dark*, featuring Dr. Guy McPherson. This is her first published book.

GUY R. McPHERSON is professor emeritus of natural resources and the environment at the University of Arizona, where he taught and conducted research for twenty award-winning years. His scholarly work, which has for many years focused on conservation of biological diversity, has produced a dozen book and hundreds of articles. Because the topics of his presentations sometimes induce despair, Guy became a certified grief-recovery specialist in January 2014. The certification came from The Grief Recovery Institute™.

CPSIA information can be obtained
at www.ICGtesting.com
Printed in the USA
FSOW02n1106211216
28754FS